喚醒你的英文語感！

Get a Feel for English !

喚醒你的英文語感！

Get a Feel for English !

翻譯大師教你讀英文

從人生故事學會用英文思考！

作者 郭岱宗

- 22 個人生必修主題，76 篇短文，閱讀能力＆人生智慧同步晉級。
- 中英短文對照，破解英文表達方式與邏輯思考關鍵差異，讓你加速讀出英文腦！

All the love on earth cannot touch the soul unless it has been expressed.

A wise man's day is worth a fool's life.

Everyone goes through hard times. What sets people apart is how they react.

貝塔語言出版
Beta Multimedia Publishing

IRT 語言測驗中心
Language Testing Center

口譯公式（The Formula of Interpreting）——郭岱宗

$$QI = EV + EK + FAAE$$

QI = **Quality Interpreting**（精於口譯）

EV = Encyclopedic Vocabulary（豐沛的字彙）

EK = Encyclopedic Knowledge（通達的見識）

F = Fluency（流暢）

流暢的字彙	流暢的句子
流暢的記憶	流暢的思路

敏捷的反應

A = Accuracy（準確）

發音準確	腔調準確
文法準確	譯意準確

A = Artistry（藝術之美）

文字之美	發音之美
語調之美	聲音之美

台風之美

E = Easiness（輕鬆自在）

金字塔理論：打造同步口譯的「金字塔」

（The Pyramid Theory of Simultaneous Interpretation）——郭岱宗

　　一切的翻譯理論，若是未能用於實際操作，都將淪為空談。優質的同步口譯超越了點、線、面，它就像一座金字塔，由下而上，用了許多石塊，每一塊都是真材實料，紮紮實實地堆砌而成。這些石塊包括了：

① 深闊的字彙

② 完整、優美、精確的譯文

③ 精簡俐落的句子

④ 迅速而正確的文法

⑤ 對雙文化貼切的掌握

⑥ 流暢的聽力

⑦ 字正腔圓

⑧ 優美愉悅的聲音

⑨ 適度的表情

⑩ 敏銳的聽眾分析和臨場反應

⑪ 穩健而親切的台風

　　最後，每一次口譯時，這些堆積的能量都隨點隨燃，立刻從金字塔的尖端爆發出來，這也就是最後一個石塊──快若子彈的速度！

　　這些石塊不但個個紮實，而且彼此緊密銜接、環環相扣、缺一不可，甚至不能鬆動。少了一角，或鬆了一塊，這個金字塔都難達高峰！

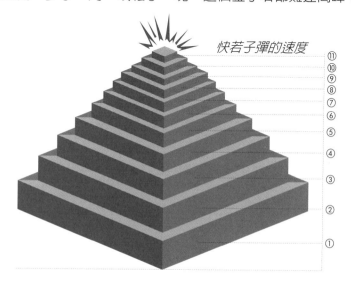

快若子彈的速度

⑪
⑩
⑨
⑧
⑦
⑥
⑤
④
③
②
①

📢 漣漪理論（Ripple Theory）+ 老鼠會方法（The Pyramid Scheme）創造龐大且紮實的字彙庫——郭岱宗

字彙範圍須用「漣漪理論」：

記背單字不應採用隨機或跳躍的方式，而應該像漣漪一樣，由近至遠，一圈一圈，緊密而廣闊。

記背方法須用快速伸展字彙的「老鼠會方法」：

平日即必須累積息息相關、深具連貫性的字彙，口譯時才能快速、精確、輕鬆、揮灑自如！「由上而下」的「老鼠會式的字彙成長」，即以一個字為原點，發展為數個字，各個字又可繼續聯想出數個字。如此，一層層下來，將可快速衍生出龐大的字彙庫。既快速、有效、又不易忘記！

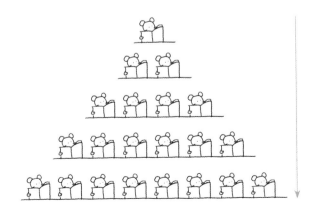

　　我看過事業成功的人自殺、看過家庭幸福的人患憂鬱症、看過美麗的女人崩潰、也看過富人的孩子痛苦。這些最有條件快樂的人，卻不見得快樂。我一直想知道，到底什麼樣的人是真正幸福的人？

　　海水不可能永遠平靜，它必時有潮水起伏；天空不可能永遠蔚藍，它必時有風起雲湧；草不可能常綠、花也不可能常開，任何的生命都必有好時、亦有壞時。既然生命如此不可測，我們所能掌握的就只有自己。

　　我終於想通了，原來真正的聰明人不是政治家、不是企業家、也非思想家，而是在順境與逆境中都能輕鬆地面帶微笑的人；而生命的贏家則是微笑至終的人。

　　如果我們能一邊閱讀英文、一邊學習用英文思考、同時一邊學習做生命的勇士和智者，豈不是一件很痛快的事？

　　這本書包含：帶著哲理的中英小短文、呼應文章的雋永諺語、可愛的插圖、還有實用的英文習題和有趣的單字遊戲，都有助於讓讀者用英文思考，請各位讀者慢慢地享用！不過，由於東西方的文化與思想不盡相同，中、英文章分別以各自的語言特色來闡述，因此，英文的部分在用字上有若干的調整，並不全然由中文逐字譯出。

　　祝福各位！願我們每一個人都能成為生命的贏家，愈活愈開心！

郭岱宗

2011 年 3 月於淡江大學

使用說明

中文和英文文章大意相同，中英文各自依照其語言習慣的說法、用詞、文化而有些許差異，並非逐字逐句直接翻譯。

只有愛？當然不夠！

婚姻就像一朵小花，每天都需要細心的呵護：

- 要用「愛」和「犧牲」來澆灌──沒有「犧牲」，就沒有真愛；沒有真愛，一切免談，根本不能結婚。
- 要用「熱情」來施肥──縱使不能常獻熱情，亦需偶而為之。
- 要用「互敬」來鬆土──言語無狀，傷害婚姻。
- 要用「溝通」來除蟲──再相知的夫妻，也需時時談心，走進對方的內心世界。
- 要用「自律」來修剪──只有愛而沒有操守的婚姻，是脆弱的。
- 要用「寬恕」來支撐──沒有人是完美的，自己當然也不完美。小事情就一笑置之吧！
- 最後，婚姻中最划算的投資，就是善待另一半的父母。

以上缺一而不可，夫妻雙方都需努力。我們縱使做不到一百分，也得有個七十分。

Words of Wisdom

Keep your eyes wide open before marriage and half-shut afterward.

Love Alone Isn't Enough

Marriage is like a tender flower that needs proper care.

- Water it with love and sacrifice[1]—true love is sacrificial.[1] Don't get married without it.
- Fertilize[2] marriage with passion—at least occasionally, if not constantly.
- Loosen the earth with respect—rude language undermines[3] marriage.
- De-worm it with communication—even the most loving couple requires good communication in order to maintain their bond.
- Trim[4] it with self-discipline—marriage with love and passion but without dignity is fragile.
- Support with forgiveness. No one is perfect. Just smile at your spouse's small mistakes.
- Finally, the most rewarding investment in a marriage is to have a good relationship with your in-laws.

All of the above are essential[5] practices for both husband and wife.

重要字彙

① sacrifice [ˈsækrəˌfaɪs] (v.) 犧牲
　sacrificial [ˌsækrəˈfɪʃəl] (adj.) 犧牲的
② fertilize [ˈfɝtḷˌaɪz] (v.) 施肥
④ undermine [ˌʌndɚˈmaɪn] (v.) 削弱基礎、逐漸損害
⑤ trim [trɪm] (v.) 修剪
⑥ essential [ɪˈsɛnʃəl] (adj.) 必要的

56　　57

呼應文章主題的智語佳句，讀者在寫作和演講時可充分運用。

英文文章中的重要字彙，附上音標、詞性和中譯。

每一章（Chapter）的最後都會有課後練習（Exercise），題型包含填充、字謎遊戲、翻譯，涵蓋本章全部內容（約包含 3~4 篇文章）的綜合練習，在有趣的練習過程中，將對這個章節的單字、用語更加深印象。

Exercise

一、填充

Marriage is like a tender flower that needs proper care:

1. F_____ it with p_____.
2. D_____ it with c_____.
3. T_____ it with s_____.
4. W_____ it with l_____ and s_____.
5. L_____ the e_____ with r_____.

二、翻譯

1. 再美的畫，如果沒有展示出來，也無法被欣賞。
   The m_____ b_____ p_____ on e_____
   cannot be s_____ unless it is d_____.

2. 再有智慧的道理，如果沒有被活出來，也只是紙上談兵。
   The w_____ p_____ on earth is w_____ if it's not
   f_____.

3. 即使老夫老妻，心中有什麼甜言蜜語，仍要說出來。
   If you have something g_____ in your h_____, e_____
   it to your s_____ n_____ m_____ y_____
   a_____.

三、Crossword Puzzles

請將以下所提示的英文單字填入字謎：

1. 惡性的 (m...t)，甩掉 (d...p)，誘惡 (s...e)，蠕覆 (r...e)，施肥 (f...e)，必要的 (e...l)

CONTENTS
目錄

Chapter 7　金錢 Money

Chapter 8　窮人與富人 The Rich and The Poor

Chapter 9　生命的意義 Significance of Life

Chapter 10　藝術 Art

Chapter 11　死亡 Death

Chapter 12　修為 Self-Possession

Chapter 13 恐懼 Fear

Chapter 14 真自由 True Freedom

Chapter 15 說話 Speech

Chapter 16 批評與建議 Criticisms

Chapter 17 面子 Due Respect

Chapter 18 交友 Friends

Chapter 19　親子 Parents and Children

Chapter 20　面對社會 Society

Chapter 21　生涯規劃 Career plan

Chapter 22　挫折 Frustrations

UNIT 1 快樂是一個習慣

如果我們要達到某一個標準才會快樂，那我們永遠不會真正快樂。

快樂不是一個標準，而是一個習慣，而且它會自動加減，因為愈快樂就愈感覺快樂；當然，愈不快樂就愈感覺不快樂。快樂的習慣一但養成，比中樂透還寶貴。我們可以什麼都沒有，但不能沒有快樂！

Words of Wisdom

Habits[5] can become second nature.

➡ 意指：習慣久了，就成了天性。

Habits Can Become Second Nature

Those who are only happy when they have a reason to be are hardly ever happy at all.

Happiness should not be conditional[1]. Instead, it should be a habit. In life, there are many things that are out of your control, but one thing you can control is yourself.

By making happiness a habit, you can maximize[2] the joy in your life and live to the fullest. Living this way should ensure[3] an existence full of joy no matter the circumstances[4].

重要字彙

① conditional [kən`dɪʃənl] (adj.) 有條件的
② maximize [`mæksə‚maɪz] (v.) 擴至最大
③ ensure [ɪn`ʃur] (v.) 確保
④ circumstance [`sɜkəm‚stæns] (n.) 環境
⑤ habit [`hæbɪt] (n.) 習慣

別用小湯匙喝水

我們如果只用小湯匙喝水,不但一時難以止渴,久了甚至會因為水喝不夠而生病。

同樣地,如果我們快樂的源頭只來自於自己的小世界,我們的心靈就如同只用小湯匙喝水,不但難以得到滋養,也會生病,常常不快樂。

把快樂的源頭擴大吧,擴大到舉目即是、每個人都可免費享有的大自然吧!宇宙中源源不盡的生命和美將使我們的靈魂永遠不乾枯。

一個微笑、一朵新開的小花、一片藍天、一聲鳥叫、一首好歌、一陣微風,都無比地好,使我們眉開眼笑,壓力頓失!

別和自己過不去了,拿個大杯子喝水吧!

Words of Wisdom

Don't seek far and wide for what lies close at hand.
➡ 意指:就在手邊,何必遠求?

Do Not Drink with a Spoon

If you are hot and thirsty but only take small sips[1] of water with a spoon, your thirst will never be quenched[2].

Similarly, if the source of your happiness comes only in small doses[3] from a small set of conditions, you will never get enough to sufficiently nourish[4] your soul.

You must broaden[5] your source for happiness! Take joy in all things, great and small. Something that provides people with almost limitless amounts of happiness is free: Nature! From colorful flowers to majestic[6] mountains to woodland[7] creatures, there is enough life and beauty in nature to keep any soul from withering[8].

A smile, a new blossom[9], a blue sky, a bird chirp[10], a beautiful song, and even a breeze[11] can cheer you up as long as you allow it to.

Don't constrain[12] yourself by sipping happiness with a spoon. Drink with a big glass!

重要字彙

① sip [sɪp] (n.) (v.) 吸

② quench [kwɛntʃ] (v.) 止渴

③ dose [dos] (n.) 劑量

④ nourish [ˈnɝɪʃ] (v.) 滋養

⑤ broaden [ˈbrɔdn̩] (v.) 加寬

⑥ majestic [məˈdʒɛstɪk] (adj.) 壯觀的

⑦ woodland [ˈwʊdˌlænd] (n.) 森林、叢林

⑧ wither [ˈwɪðə] (v.) 枯萎

⑨ blossom [ˈblɑsəm] (n.) 花朵

⑩ chirp [tʃɝp] (n.) (v.) 鳥叫聲

⑪ breeze [briz] (n.) 微風

⑫ constrain [kənˈstren] (v.) 抑制

愈愛比較，愈不快樂

許多好東西超越了物質界的價值：

鑽石亮？還是星星亮？都亮！

珍珠美？還是水滴美？都美！

翡翠綠？還是嫩葉綠？都綠！

紅寶紅？還是玫瑰紅？都紅！

燕窩嫩？還是豆花嫩？都嫩！

牛排好吃？還是牛肉麵好吃？都好吃！

快樂來自心境與胸懷。知足常樂！

Words of Wisdom

Every woman needs two men—one to be married to and the other to compare with.

Which Is More Valuable?

. . . .

Diamonds are dazzling, so are stars!

Pearls[1] are elegant, so are water drops!

Jade[2] is green, so are tender leaves!

Rubies[3] are red, so are roses!

★

Sometimes the most valuable things in life are free!

★ 以翻譯的角度來說，燕窩（swallow's nest）、豆花（tofu pudding）、牛肉麵
（beef noodles）不適合用在此文，因為西方人對這些食物和它們的價錢較不熟
悉。

重要字彙

① pearl [pɜl] (n.) 珍珠
② jade [dʒed] (n.) 玉
③ ruby [ˈrubɪ] (n.) 紅寶石

一、填充

A.

1. 你喝這麼一小瓶水，怎麼止渴？

How can you q_____ your t_____ with such a small

bottle of water?

2. 你心情天天這麼惡劣，靈魂如何得到滋養？

How can you n_____ your soul if you're this u_____ all

the time?

3. 這朵花正逐漸枯萎。

This flower is w_____.

4. 我可以喝一口你的珍珠奶茶嗎？

Can I t_____ a s_____ of your b_____

t_____?

5. 我的父母供給我充分的錢。

My parents s_____ p_____ me with money.

B. 請填入和左邊一樣美麗，卻不用花錢的東西

6. diamonds — 　
7. pearls — 　
8. jade — 　
9. rubies —

二、Crossword Puzzles

請將以下單字的英文填入字謎：

1. 有條件的 (c...l)，擴至最大 (m...e)，確保 (e...e)，環境 (c...e)，
   習慣 (h...t)

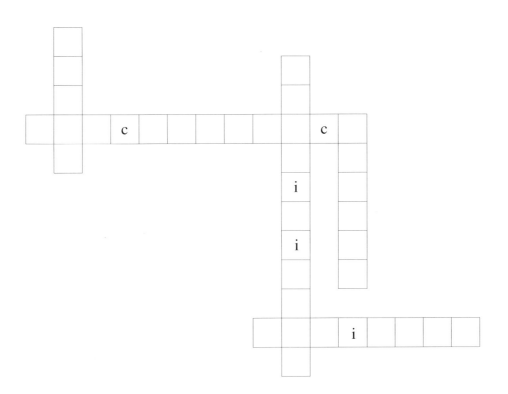

2. 鑽石 (d...d)，珍珠 (p...l)，水「珠」(d...p)，玉 (j...e)，紅寶 (r...y)，
   枯萎 (w...r)

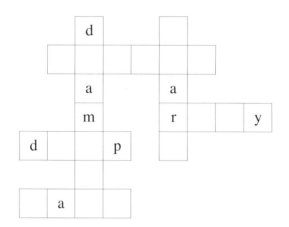

答案

一、填充

1. quench, thirst
2. nourish, upset
3. withering
4. take, sip, bubble tea
5. sufficiently provide

6. stars
7. water drops
8. tender leaves
9. roses

二、Crossword Puzzles

1. **Across** circumstance, maximize

   Down habit, conditional, ensure
2. **Across** wither, ruby, drop, jade

   Down diamond, pearl

愈感恩，愈有福氣！

即使日子難過，但是如果能夠時時感恩，就會發現，人生實在是美好的：

一早起床時，心中感恩──許多人昨晚一覺不起！

一大早趕著上班，心中感恩──許多人沒有工作！

被劈腿了，心中感恩──重獲自由，重新出發！

身體不舒服──這表示我們還活著，有生命就感恩！

感恩不是富人的專利。我們只要開始數算自己所擁有的，就知道我們是多麼地富裕。愈感恩，愈有福氣！

Words of Wisdom

豐盛　　　　　　　　　　　　　　　　　滿足
Abundance doesn't know contentment, but contentment knows abundance.

Contentment[1] Brings Happiness

In good times or bad, count your blessings.[2]

The first thing you should be in the morning when you get up is thankful[3]—there are people out there who didn't make it through the night.

Have to rush to work? Be thankful—lots of people are jobless.[4]

Recently broke up with your significant other? Be thankful—you're free again to find a new love! *

Not feeling well? Be thankful—where there's life, there's hope!

Gratefulness is not reserved[5] for the rich. Once you start appreciating what you already have, you'll be amazed at how rich your life really is.

* 劈腿（two-time）或劈腿者（two timer）是罵人的話，在此不適合譯出，因為它們和這一句開導人的意境不同。

重要字彙

① contentment [kən`tɛntmənt] (n.) 滿足
② blessing [`blɛsɪŋ] (n.) 祝福
③ thankful [`θæŋkfəl] (adj.) 感恩
④ jobless [`dʒablɪs] (adj.) 失業中
⑤ reserve [rɪ`zɜv] (v.) 保留

自怨自艾的人最貧窮！

別人不能摧毀我們，只有自己才可以徹底地打倒自己。

人生都有苦難，只是形式不同，所以不要自艾自憐。

美國盲人作家海倫凱勒（Helen Keller）所朝思暮想的就是重見光明三天，「三天」而已！她渴望見到溫暖的陽光──陽光到底是什麼樣子？她渴望見到愛她的人──他們的眼神是如何？

我們這輩子都看得見的人，如果只看見了自己的不幸和缺乏，就辜負了造物者所賜給我們的眼睛。

心盲比眼盲更可悲，因為這樣的人永遠看不到自己的富有，是真正的窮人！

Words of Wisdom

An ungrateful man is a tub full of holes.

浴缸

Don't Wallow[1] in Self-Pity

Sometimes we can be our own worst enemies.

Frustrations[2] and difficulties are a part of life. Reacting to them with self-pity[3] is unhealthy and unproductive.[4]

The American writer Helen Keller's biggest dream was simply to be able to see for three days. Just three days! She longed for nothing more than the ability to experience the color of a sunset and see the eyes of the people who loved her.

For those of us who have had the gift of sight our entire lives, it would truly be a shame if we only used that precious gift to see our own misfortunes[5] and inadequacies.[6]

重要字彙

① wallow [ˈwɑlo] (v.) 陷入泥沼
② frustration [ˌfrʌsˈtreʃən] (n.) 挫敗
③ self-pity [ˈsɛlfˈpɪtɪ] (n.) 自憐
④ unproductive [ˌʌnprəˈdʌktɪv] (adj.) 沒有意義的、無用的
⑤ misfortune [mɪsˈfɔrtʃən] (n.) 不幸
⑥ inadequacy [ɪnˈædəkwəsɪ] (n.) 不足
    inadequate [ɪnˈædəkwɪt] (adj.) 不足

Crossword Puzzles

請將以下所提示的英文單字填入字謎：

1. 祝福 (b...g)，感恩的 (t...l)，無業的 (j...s)，保留 (r...e)，滿足 (c...t)

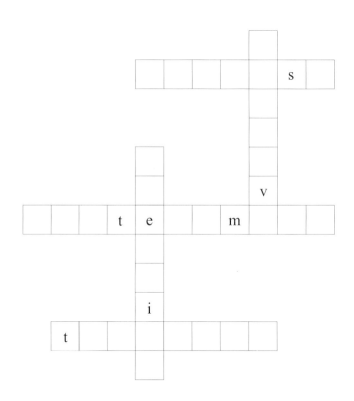

2. 陷入 (w...w)，不幸之事 (m...e)，不幸的 (u...e)，不足的 (i...e)，驚喜的
(a...d)

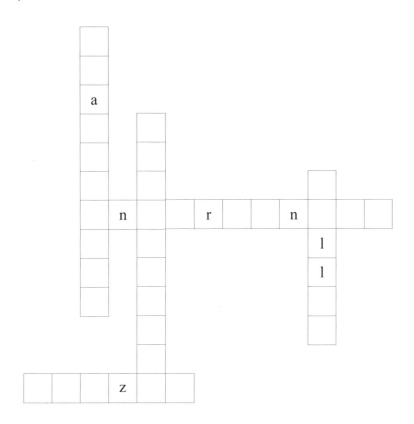

 答案

1. **Across** jobless, contentment, thankful
   Down blessing, reserve
2. **Across** unfortunate, amazed
   Down inadequate, misfortune, wallow

靈體分離

為了跟上社會的脈動，我們經常是忙碌的。如果我們能學會將心靈與身體分離，就可避開許多痛苦。否則，長久下來，小自壓力、大至恐慌，可能都會找上我們。

我們的心，應該經常是寧靜的：
即使我們外表在辯論，其實靈魂是安靜的。
即使我們外表在工作，其實靈魂是休息的。
即使我們外表在趕車，其實靈魂是靜態的。
最不容易的是，即使我們外表在受苦，其實靈魂是平靜的。

靈體必須分離。許多演員下了戲，心靈仍難以平復，飽受煎熬，就是靈體未分的極端例子。

Words of Wisdom

In a calm sea, every person is a pilot.
➡ 意指：任何人在平靜中都能平穩駕駛。

Isolate[1] Our Souls

In today's hectic[2] society, anxiety[3] and stress are a common part of our lives. If we could learn to isolate our minds from our bodies, we could relieve[4] pressure and bring calm to our lives.

Our minds should be continuously[5] peaceful:
Our minds should be calm while we are debating[6] with people.
Our minds should be peaceful while we are working.
Our minds should feel at ease while we are trying to catch the bus.
Our minds should be serene[7] even when our bodies suffer.

We must learn to separate ourselves from our troubles.

重要字彙

① isolate [ˈaɪslˌet] (v.) 分離
② hectic [ˈhɛktɪk] (adj.) 汲汲營營的
③ anxiety [æŋˈzaɪətɪ] (n.) 焦慮
④ relieve [rɪˈliv] (v.) 解脫
⑤ continuously [kənˈtɪnjuəslɪ] (adv.) 持續地
⑥ debate [dɪˈbet] (v.) 辯論
⑦ serene [səˈrin] (adj.) 寧靜的

不要求公平

　　有時候，壞人會逢好事，好人也會遭遇壞事。要求公平，會使我們暴躁，請不要心存這種期盼：

　　我們開車守規矩，但不期望別人和我們一樣，否則我們難免暴躁。

　　我們對朋友講義氣，但不期望朋友會對我們一樣，否則我們難免憤恨不平。

　　我們幫助人，但不期待別人同樣回報我們，否則我們難免生氣。

　　不必要求公平，因為天下沒有完全的公平。即使最平的鏡子，在放大鏡下，也有凸凹。

　　內心的寧靜比被公平對待重要。

Words of Wisdom

Everyone likes justice in another's home, but none in his or her own.

Do Not Expect to Be Fairly Treated

Sometimes good things happen to bad people and vice-versa.[1] Expecting absolute fairness in life will only lead to anger and disappointment.

When driving in the street, do not expect other drivers to be polite.

When doing something nice for a friend, do not expect him or her to return the favor.

When we help people, we should not expect anything in return. Instead, take satisfaction in the good deed[2] itself.

Absolute fairness does not exist. The surface of even the smoothest mirror looks uneven[3] under a magnifying scope.[4]

Be at peace with the nature of the world and enjoy it for what it is.

重要字彙

① vice-versa [ˌvaɪsɪˋvɝsə] (*adv.*) 反之亦然
② deed [did] (*n.*) 行為
③ uneven [ʌnˋivən] (*adj.*) 凹凸不平的
④ magnifying scope [skop] (*n.*) 放大鏡

UNIT 8 和自己面對面

我們會整理儀容，也會整理房子。但是，有多久沒有整理心靈了？它仍健康嗎？

和自己面對面：

——我們的生活節奏太快了嗎？放慢腳步吧！

——我們生活有些萎靡嗎？振作起來吧！

——我們的心太容易受傷了嗎？瀟灑一些吧！

——我們易怒難平嗎？多些寬厚吧！

——我們容易恐懼嗎？勇敢一點吧！

找回那個平靜的自己吧！

Words of Wisdom

Calmness is a great advantage.

　　　　　好處

Look Into Ourselves

• •

Everyone uses a mirror to make sure that he or she looks good.

We regularly clean our houses so that we can live in a good environment, but how often do we look into our souls and see what needs to change?

Are you living an unhealthily fast life? Slow it down!

Are you often dejected?[1] Cheer up!

Are you easily hurt? Be strong!

Do you often lose your temper? Stay cool!

Are you going through a rough patch?[2] Be brave!

Find that peaceful soul!

重要字彙

① dejected [dɪˋdʒɛktɪd] (*adj.*) 萎靡的
② rough patch [rʌf pætʃ] (*n.*) 難關

UNIT 9 享受孤獨

在激流中，水來到深處時，自然平靜下來。

人也一樣，在平日的混亂之後，如果來到內心深處，就能享受那一份完全屬於自己的寧靜。**寧靜中更有智慧。**

孤獨是一種休閒，我們偶而應該孤獨。先放空自己——沒有工作、沒有朋友、沒有兒女、沒有疾病、沒有恐懼、沒有慾望、甚至沒有喜樂、沒有明天。

淺淺的小溪沒有能量，深而靜的水庫才能為未來貯存能量。我們要享受孤獨，因為**寧靜致遠。**

Words of Wisdom

Solitude is the nurse of wisdom.

Enjoy Solitude

. . . .

In a rushing stream[1], water flows slowly in the deepest places.

When living a hectic life, calming down and being alone is the only way to achieve self-enlightenment[2] and tranquility.[3] Wisdom grows in tranquility.

Occasional moments of solitude[4] are like a vacation. To achieve this, try to empty yourself of all worries, thoughts, and distractions.[5]

Shallow[6] streams have no power. Only deep and quiet reservoirs[7] can accumulate[8] power. Enjoy your solitude. Sometimes doing so is the only way to find yourself.

重要字彙

① rushing stream [ˈrʌʃɪŋ strim] (n.) 湍急的溪流
② enlightenment [ɪnˈlaɪtn̩mənt] (n.) 啟發
　 enlighten [ɪnˈlaɪtn̩] (v.) 啟發
③ tranquility [træŋˈkwɪlətɪ] (n.) 寧靜
　 tranquil [ˈtræŋkwɪl] (adj.) 寧靜的
④ solitude [ˈsɑləˌtjud] (n.) 獨處
⑤ distraction [dɪˈstrækʃən] (n.) 分心
　 distracted [dɪˈstræktɪd] (adj.) 分心的
⑥ shallow [ˈʃælo] (adj.) 淺的
⑦ reservoir [ˈrɛzəˌvɔr] (n.) 水庫
⑧ accumulate [əˈkjumjəˌlet] (v.) 累積

一、填充

請填入以下動作的目的：

動作	功效
1. We use a mirror	
2. We clean our houses	
3. We look into our souls	

請填入發生以下狀況時，我們應該如何自我調整：

4. living an unhealthy fast life ⸺ [_____]

5. often dejected ⸺ [_____]

6. easily hurt ⸺ [_____]

7. often losing one's temper ⸺ [_____]

8. going through a rough patch ⸺ [_____]

二、翻譯

1. 在激流中，水來到深處時，自然平靜下來。

   In a r_____ s_____, w_____ f_____ slowly

   in the d_____ p_____.

2. 寧靜中更有智慧。

   W_____ g_____ in t_____.

3. 偶爾孤獨，是一種休閒。

O_____ m_____ of s_____ are like a v_____.

4. 淺的小溪沒能量。

S_____ s_____ have no p_____.

5. 只有深而靜的水庫才能貯存能量。

O_____ d_____ and q_____ r_____ can

a_____ p_____.

三、Crossword Puzzle

請將以下所提示的英文單字填入字謎：使孤立 (i...e)，焦慮 (a...y)，解除
(r...e)，不斷地 (c...y)，辯論 (d...e)，寧靜的 (s...e)，行為 (d...d)

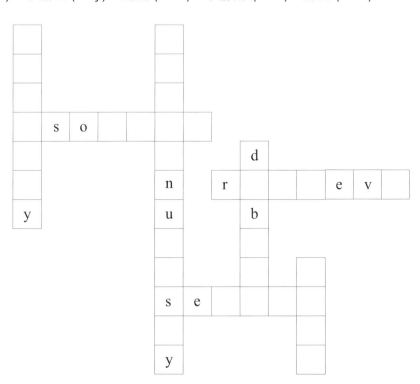

答案

一、填充

1. to make sure that we look good.

2. so that we can live in a nice environment.

3. to see what needs to change.

4. Slow it down!

5. Cheer up!

6. Be strong!

7. Stay cool!

8. Be brave!

二、翻譯

1. rushing stream, water flows, deepest places

2. Wisdom grows, tranquility

3. Occasional moments, solitude, vacation

4. Shallow streams, power

5. Only deep, quiet reservoirs, accumulate power

三、Crossword Puzzle

Across isolate, relieve, serene

Down anxiety, continuously, debate, deed

Notes

UNIT 10 早比晚好

會背叛我們的人，遲早都會背叛，而且今天背叛我們，以後事情可能會重演。這種人就像一個臭瘤，愈早發現愈好，而且趕快把它割掉，丟得遠遠的，絕對不要再拿來聞！

不要怕失戀，因為：
——現在發生，比我們感情陷得更深時才發現要好！
——婚前發生又比婚後發現的好！
——婚後尚未生育的時候發生，當然比有了孩子才發生要好！
——在我們三十歲的時候背叛我們，又比等到我們四十歲了、已入中年時再背叛要好！
——當然，在我們四十歲背叛我們，又比在我們衰老虛弱、難以招架之時再背叛要好！

天下沒什麼新鮮事，什麼都可以泰然處之。

Words of Wisdom

A leopard can't change its spots.
　　　　　花豹　　　　　　　　　　斑點
➡ 意指：本性難改。

44

Better Earlier Than Later!

. . . .

Someone who betrays[1] you once will most likely do it again. This kind of person is just like a malignant[2] tumor, which should be removed as early as possible.

Do not be afraid of failing in love. If someone is going to betray you, it's better to have it happen earlier rather than later.

Already in a relationship? Better now than when you fall more deeply in love.

Already deeply in love? Better now than after you're married.

Already married? Better now than after you've had children.

Already have children? Better now than after you're too old to have a second chance.

Good and bad things happen all the time. Just take them in stride.[3]

※ 年齡對西方女人來說,是很敏感的事,尤其是三、四十歲之時,所以在此不用提。

重要字彙

① betray [bɪ`tre] (v.) 背叛
② malignant [mə`lɪgnənt] (adj.) 惡性的
③ in stride [ɪn straɪd] 從容自在

散場了就走人

　　我們不要放大失戀的痛苦。一切的歡笑和眼淚都過去了，就像看了一場電影，散場了就走吧，沒人會看完了電影還待在電影院裏，日夜流連而不離去的。

　　不須為已經不愛我們的人流半滴眼淚！人生的變化太大也太快，凡事不須執著，也不要害怕。

　　人生本如戲，散場了就走人吧。

Words of Wisdom

I would rather be betrayed than betray because there is karma.

因果報應

Let Go!

· ·

It's no big deal to fail in love. An ended relationship is just like seeing a movie. Whether laughter or tears, good times or bad, all things have passed. After the movie is over, leave the theater and go home. There is no point in staying after the show is over.

Do not shed a single tear for someone who doesn't love you any more. Life is short. Don't waste it being unhappy.

Life is like a show. When the show ends, go home.

 **現實勝於回憶**

失戀時，最大的殺傷力是回憶。因為失戀時所想念的經常都只是美好的片段。

當我們有以下回憶時，不妨面對現實：

回憶：他以前好貼心。

現實：但是他現在不貼心啊！

回憶：他下雨天還來接我，把我顧得好好的。

現實：重點是，現在下雨了，他在哪兒？

回憶：她常像小鳥一樣，躺在我懷裡。

現實：她現在躺在別人懷裡，這樣的人你還寄望什麼呢？

回憶：他很老實，是被那個女孩子騙走了！

現實：那是他的事。他不替你想，你還替他想得那麼周全？

Words of Wisdom

Without suffering, there's no life.

➡ 意指：生命力必由冶煉而來。

Reality Is More Important Than Memories

One of the most painful things about being dumped[1] is being left with memories of better times. But one must realize that memories do not exist in reality.

Memory: He was so sweet.

Reality: He dumped you. That's not sweet at all!

Memory: He picked me up when it rained. He always took good care of me.

Reality: It's raining now, and he's not coming for you.

Memory: She used to cuddle in my arms like a little bird.

Reality: She's doing the same thing in someone else's arms.

Memory: He wasn't the one who betrayed me. It was the girl who seduced[2] him.

Reality: He is responsible for his own actions. Don't make excuses for someone who doesn't care about you.

重要字彙

① dump [dʌmp] (v.) 甩掉、拋棄
② seduce [sɪˋdjus] (v.) 誘惑

UNIT 13　遭受背叛不全然是壞事

天啊！我們全心全意所愛的人居然愛上了別人？先別慌，靜下心來，我們可以從以下幾個反應中做出選擇：

1. 如果我們痛苦、失眠、憤怒——傷了自己，也傷了父母。「身體髮膚，受之父母。」不可毀傷！

2. 如果我們委屈求全、執意挽回，盼他（她）心回意轉——自取其辱、延伸痛苦、自掘墳墓！

3. 如果我們到處訴苦——何必一再重溫不快樂的事，跟自己過不去，也讓身邊的人不好過？

我們可以喝杯茶、看場電影、慶祝重獲自由——**我要比他（她）過得更好！**

Words of Wisdom

延長

One moment of intense happiness prolongs life a thousand years.
➡ 意指：「快樂」很重要！

Being Cheated On Isn't That Bad

Nothing can be more heartbreaking than when our sweetheart falls in love with someone else. Don't panic. Things aren't that bad:

1. Feel angry or hurt? Can't sleep at night? You're only hurting yourself.
2. Want to try and win your partner back? You're only setting yourself up for more heartbreak.
3. Can't stop talking about your pain? Dwelling[1] on unpleasant things makes those around you uncomfortable and makes it harder to put those things behind you.

Have a cup of tea, see a movie, and celebrate your new freedom. Living well is the best revenge![2]

重要字彙

① dwell [dwɛl] (*v.*) 停留在某種狀態
② revenge [rɪ`vɛndʒ] (*n.*)(*v.*) 報仇

Exercise

一、填充

1. 不要怕失戀。

   Don't be afraid of f_____ in l_____.

2. 這種人就像一個毒瘤，早拿走早好。

   This kind of person is just like a m_____ t_____ w_____

   sh_____ b_____ r_____ as e_____ as

   possible.

3. 天下沒什麼新鮮事，好事壞事都要泰然處之。

   G_____ and b_____ t_____ h_____ all

   the time. Just t_____ them i_____ s_____.

4. 所有的歡笑和淚水都會過去。

   A_____ t_____ l_____ and t_____

   w_____ pass.

5. 電影結束了，待在那兒沒意義！

   There is n_____ p_____ i_____ s_____

   after the s_____ is o_____.

6. 不要為不再愛你的人流半滴淚。

   Don't s_____ a s_____ t_____ for someone who

   doesn't love you any more.

7. 被拋棄時，最痛苦的事情，就是回憶。

   One of the most p_____ things about b_____ d_____

is b_____ l_____ w_____ memories.

8. 他甩了她！

    He d_____ her!

9. 如果下雨，我去接你。

    I'll p_____ you u_____ if i_____ r_____.

10. 她像小鳥一樣依偎在他懷裡。

    She c_____ i_____ his a_____ like a little bird.

11. 她在引誘他!

    She is s_____ him!

12. 這真令人心碎！

    This is h_____!

13. 別慌！

    Don't p_____!

14. 重溫不快樂的事情，使人難以擺脫痛苦！

    Dw_____ o_____ unpleasant things m_____ it
    h_____ to p_____ t_____ p_____ b_____
    you.

15. 活得好，是最好的報復。

    L_____ w_____ is the best r_____!

16. 被劈腿是化了妝的祝福。

    B_____ c_____ o_____ is a b_____
    i_____ d_____.

答案

一、填充

1. failing, love

2. malignant tumor which should be removed, early

3. Good, bad things happen, take, in stride

4. All the laughter, tears will

5. no point in staying, show, over

6. shed, single tear

7. painful, being dumped, being left with

8. dumped

9. pick, up, it rains

10. cuddles in, arms

11. seducing

12. heartbreaking

13. panic

14. Dwelling on, makes, hard, put the pain behind

15. Living well, revenge

16. Being cheated on, blessing in disguise

Notes

UNIT 14　只有愛？當然不夠！

婚姻就像一朵小花，每天都需要細心的呵護：

- 要用「愛」和「犧牲」來澆灌——沒有「犧牲」，就沒有真愛；沒有真愛，一切免談，根本不能結婚。
- 要用「熱情」來施肥——縱使不能常獻熱情，亦需偶而為之。
- 要用「互敬」來鬆土——言語無狀，傷害婚姻。
- 要用「溝通」來除蟲——再相知的夫妻，也需時時談心，走進對方的內心世界。
- 要用「自律」來修剪——只有愛而沒有操守的婚姻，是脆弱的。
- 要用「寬恕」來支撐——沒有人是完美的，自己當然也不完美。小事情就一笑置之吧！
- 最後，婚姻中最划算的投資，就是善待另一半的父母。

以上缺一而不可，夫妻雙方都需努力。我們縱使做不到一百分，也得有個七十分。

Words of Wisdom

Keep your eyes wide open before marriage and half-shut afterward.

Love Alone Isn't Enough

. . . .

Marriage is like a tender flower that needs proper care.

- **Water it with love and sacrifice[1]—true love is sacrificial.[1] Don't get married without it.**
- **Fertilize[2] marriage with passion—at least occasionally, if not constantly.**
- **Loosen the earth with respect—rude language undermines[3] marriage.**
- **De-worm it with communication—even the most loving couple requires good communication in order to maintain their bond.**
- **Trim[4] with self-discipline—marriage with love and passion but without dignity is fragile.**
- **Support with forgiveness. No one is perfect. Just smile at your spouse's small mistakes.**
- **Finally, the most rewarding investment in a marriage is to have a good relationship with your in-laws.**

All of the above are essential[5] practices for both husband and wife.

重要字彙

① sacrifice [ˈsækrəˌfaɪs] (v.) 犧牲
sacrificial [ˌsækrəˈfɪʃəl] (adj.) 犧牲的
② fertilize [ˈfɝtḷˌaɪz] (v.) 施肥

③ undermine [ˌʌndɚˈmaɪn] (v.) 削弱基礎、逐漸損害
④ trim [trɪm] (v.) 修剪
⑤ essential [ɪˈsɛnʃəl] (adj.) 必要的

UNIT 15 說出真心話

情侶或夫妻之間的表達很重要：

——聯絡不到另一半時，與其質問對方：「你躲到哪裡了？和誰一起？做了什麼？」不如說出真心話：「我找不到你，心裏很著急，怕你發生了什麼事。」

——另一半言語傷到了你，與其說：「你幹麻講這種話？很過分耶！」不如說出真心話：「你這樣說話，我心裏好難受，因為我很在乎你。」

只要有真愛，就可以說出心裏真正在乎的是什麼。

Words of Wisdom

A soft answer calms the wrath.

憤怒

Say What You Really Mean

. . . .

Proper communication between husband and wife is important. For example, instead of interrogating[1] a spouse with questions like "Where did you go?" or "Who were you with?" say "I was worried and didn't know what happened to you."

When a spouse's language has hurt you, instead of saying "Who do you think you're talking to?" you can say, "I feel so hurt to hear this from you because I care about what you say."

Where love is concerned,[2] open and honest communication is always the best policy.

重要字彙

① interrogate [ɪn`tɛrəˌget] (v.) 質詢
② concerned [kən`sɜnd] (adj.) 有關的

甜言蜜語不可少

再美的一幅畫，如果沒有被展示出來，也無法被欣賞。

再動人的一首歌，如果沒有被唱出來，也沒人聆聽。

再有智慧的哲理，如果沒有被活出來，也是紙上談兵。

再多的愛，如果沒有被表達出來，也無法碰觸靈魂。

人的感官是多方面的，僅視力所及，是不夠的。

即使老夫老妻，甜言蜜語仍深觸心靈。

「謝謝！」

「對不起！」

「感謝你包容我的缺點。」

「你在我心目中，是最美的！」

「能嫁給你是我的榮幸！」

「我一輩子愛你！」

Words of Wisdom

The tongue can paint what the eyes can't see.

➡ 意指：言語很重要。

Express the Good Things in Your Heart

• •

The most beautiful painting on earth cannot be seen unless it is displayed.

The most beautiful song on earth cannot be heard unless it is sung.

The wisest philosophy[1] on earth is worthless if it isn't followed.

All the love on earth cannot touch the soul unless it has been expressed.

If you have something good in your heart, express it to your spouse no matter your age.

重要字彙

① philosophy [fə`lɑsəfɪ] (*n.*) 哲學

UNIT 17 愛情是什麼？

只要認真經營婚姻，我們可以談一輩子的戀愛：

■ 年少時的愛情，像一顆生澀的青蘋果——所以淺嚐即止，不須太過執著。

■ 成年時的愛情，像一朵綻放的紅玫瑰，浪漫誘人——所以盡心享受，開始經營。

■ 中年時的愛情，像一杯濃醇的咖啡，香郁芬芳——所以要輕聲細語，慢慢品嚐。

■ 老年時的愛情，像一杯最尊貴的美酒——只要熱情 + 愛情 + 親情 = 100分，就十分圓滿了。

只要用心，我們從年少到年老，可以和另一半談一輩子的戀愛。

Words of Wisdom

Marriage is like buying melons—you need a little luck.

What's Love Like?

. . . .

Love can last forever, but it must be managed correctly.

■ Teenage romance[1] can be passionate but is not often based on a solid foundation.[2]

■ Romance in young adults is more substantial,[3] but it can take effort to ensure that it lasts.

■ Middle-age romance is like a mellow[4] coffee—after a bit of work has been put in, it can be slowly savored.[5]

■ Romance at an old age is like a fine wine—deep, complex, and uniquely satisfying because it is interwoven[6] with family, history, and memories.

If you want, you can be in love with your spouse[7] forever.

重要字彙

① romance [ro`mæns] (n.) 浪漫
② foundation [faʊn`deʃən] (n.) 基礎
③ substantial [səb`stænʃəl] (adj.) 真實的
④ mellow [`mɛlo] (adj.) (v.) 圓熟的
⑤ savor [`sevə] (v.) 品嚐
⑥ interweave [ˌɪntə`wiv] (v.) 使混雜、交織
⑦ spouse [spaʊz] (n.) 配偶

一、填充

Marriage is like a tender flower that needs proper care:

1. F_____ it with p_____.

2. D_____ it with c_____.

3. T_____ it with s_____.

4. W_____ it with l_____ and s_____.

5. L_____ the e_____ with r_____.

二、翻譯

1. 再美的畫，如果沒有展示出來，也無法被欣賞。

The m_____ b_____ p_____ on e_____

cannot be s_____ unless it is d_____.

2. 再有智慧的哲理，如果沒有被活出來，也只是紙上談兵。

The w_____ p_____ on earth is w_____ if it's not

f_____.

3. 即使老夫老妻，心中有什麼甜言蜜語，仍要說出來。

If you have something g_____ in your h_____, e_____

it to your s_____ n_____ m_____ y_____

a_____.

三、Crossword Puzzles

請將以下所提示的英文單字填入字謎：

1. 惡性的 (m...t)，甩掉 (d...p)，誘惑 (s...e)，報復 (r...e)，施肥 (f...e)，必
   要的 (e...l)

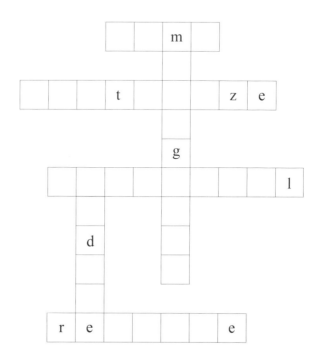

2. 基礎 (f...n)，愛情 (r...e)，真實的 (s...l)，圓熟的 (m...w)，品嚐 (s...r)，
   交織 (i...e)，配偶 (s...e)

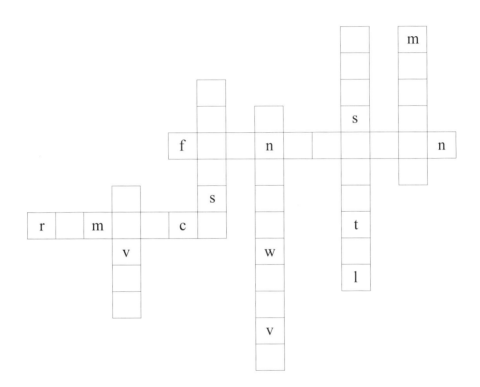

答案

一、填充

1. Fertilize, passion

2. De-worm, communication

3. Trim, self-discipline

4. Water, love, sacrifice

5. Loosen, earth, respect

二、翻譯

1. most beautiful painting, earth, seen, displayed

2. wisest philosophy, worthless, followed

3. good, heart, express, spouse no matter your age

三、Crossword Puzzles

1. **Across** dump, fertilize, essential, revenge

   Down seduce, malignant

2. **Across** foundation, romance

   Down savor, spouse, interweave, substantial, mellow

UNIT 18 管好嘴巴

聖經有句話：「溫柔的舌頭，可以折斷骨頭。」

舌頭是一個又軟又小的器官，它卻可以造就一個人，也可以摧毀一個人，我們說話不可不慎。

同一個嘴巴，可以說出謙柔、誠摯、溫暖、助人的言語，也可以說出惡毒、虛假、驕傲、傷人的言語。在這大量溝通的世界裡，我們如果能夠管好嘴巴，就已成功了一半！

Words of Wisdom

The tongue talks at the head's cost.
➡ 意指：舌頭說錯話，可能要掉腦袋。

Control Your Tongue

• •

A wise saying in the Bible states, "A soft tongue can break bones."

It is easy to forget that words can be as powerful as bullets[1] and swords.[2] Words can build up or destroy a person.

From the same mouth, humble, warm, and sincere language can be spoken along with mean, hypocritical,[3] and arrogant[4] language. It is up to you to choose what kind of person you want to be.

In this world of easy-to-use mass communication, someone who can control his or her tongue is already a step ahead.

> 重要字彙

① bullet [ˋbʊlɪt] (n.) 子彈
② sword [sord] (n.) 劍
③ hypocritical [͵hɪpəˋkrɪtɪkl̩] (adj.) 偽善的
④ arrogant [ˋærəgənt] (adj.) 傲慢的

好氣質最迷人

氣質裝不出來，因為它不是一時的。好氣質像一瓶美酒，時間愈久愈醉人。

好氣質必有安定的眼神，而安定的眼神來自平靜的心。
好氣質必有溫暖的微笑，而溫暖的微笑來自喜樂的心。
好氣質必有堅定的自信，而堅定的自信來自自我充實。
好氣質必有從容的舉止，而從容的舉止來自緩慢的呼吸。
好氣質必有一顆柔軟的心，因為我們一生的形象都由心發出。

Words of Wisdom

Without grace, beauty is an unbaited hook.
➡ 意指：美麗若缺乏優雅，就像一個沒餌的魚鉤，毫無吸引力。

Temperament and Disposition

• •

A person's temperament[1] and disposition[2] is an essential part of his or her character. Like good wine, these qualities only get better with age.

A good disposition is one that is peaceful, gentle, cheerful, and confident. Someone with all of these attributes[3] will display them through his or her eyes, smile, and actions.

You can not always control the world around you, but you can control the way you act and react to the things that happen to you.

A good disposition does not exist without a kind heart.

重要字彙

---

① temperament [ˈtɛmprəmənt] (n.) 性情
② disposition [ˌdɪspəˈzɪʃən] (n.) 氣質
③ attribute [əˈtrɪbjut] (n.) 品性、屬性

UNIT 20 慈眉善目

我們無論言語如何，眼睛是騙不了人的。

──眼神閃爍不定的，不可交，因為不知道他在打什麼主意。

──眼神曖昧不明的，不可交，因為他不誠懇。

──眼神冷酷遙遠的，不可交，因為我們和他難有交集。

──眼神兇惡的，不可交，因為他會拿走我們心中的平靜。

──**眉目慈善的人，心中有愛，非常地吸引人。**

Words of Wisdom

A gentle disposition is like an unruffled stream.

沒被擾亂的

The Eyes Are The Windows to the Soul

The eyes don't deceive.[1]

Do not believe those whose eyes are not stable because you never know what they're up to.

Do not believe those whose eyes are ambiguous[2] because they may not be sincere.

Do not believe those whose eyes are cold and remote[3] because they may not be willing to share.

Do not believe those whose eyes are vicious[4] because they may take away your peace of mind.

Those who have merciful[5] eyes are attractive because they have love in their hearts.

重要字彙

① deceive [dɪ`siv] (v.) 欺騙
② ambiguous [æm`bɪgjʊəs] (adj.) 曖昧不明的
③ remote [rɪ`mot] (adj.) 冷漠的
④ vicious [`vɪʃəs] (adj.) 邪惡的
⑤ merciful [`mɜsɪfəl] (adj.) 慈悲的

節奏收放自如

我們做什麼，都要從容卻有效：

——我們工作的時候全神投入，不要左顧右盼，因為認真工作的人受人尊敬。

——我們工作要注重效率，不要輕易地被耽擱，因為有高效率的人很吸引人。

——當我們工作完畢，要徹底而盡快地回歸自己，才能開始慢活。收放自如的人很吸引人。

——我們要學習一種可以隨時拔腿追搭巴士，也可以隨時坐下來閱讀的功夫。內心不被外界牽引的人很吸引人。

——該快的時候快，該慢的時候慢，**能夠氣定神閒地掌握生活節奏的人，真的很吸引人。**

Words of Wisdom

If the rhythm of the drum beat changes, the dance step must adapt.

節奏　　　　　　　拍子　　　　　　　　　　調整

Be Flexible[1]

· ·

While it is generally good to be cool and efficient,[2] one should adjust one's tempo[3] to his or her surroundings.

People who devote[4] their full concentration at work are rewarded,[5] but those who are too serious or focused, even outside of the office, are poor companions.[6]

After work it is important to relax and be yourself.

To live an efficient life, it is important to be able to run your fastest to catch a bus in one moment, then calm down and read quietly the next.

Those who are able to freely and easily control their tempo of life have a certain charisma and significant advantage[7] over those who can not.

重要字彙

① flexible [ˋflɛksəbl] (*adj.*) 可彎曲的
② efficient [ɪˋfɪʃənt] (*adj.*) 有效率的
③ tempo [ˋtɛmpo] (*n.*) 節拍
④ devote [dɪˋvot] (*v.*) 付出
⑤ reward [rɪˋwɔrd] (*v.*)(*n.*) 回報
⑥ companion [kəmˋpænjən] (*n.*) 同伴
⑦ advantage [ədˋvæntɪdʒ] (*n.*) 優勢

一、填充

1. A peaceful look comes from a p＿＿＿＿＿ h＿＿＿＿＿.

2. Gentle smiles come from a ch＿＿＿＿＿ h＿＿＿＿＿.

3. Unshakable confidence comes from s＿＿＿＿＿-f＿＿＿＿＿.

4. Easiness comes from s＿＿＿＿＿ b＿＿＿＿＿.

Be aware of those whose

5. eyes are not stable.   →   *You never know what they're up to.*

6. eyes are ambiguous.   →   ＿＿＿＿＿＿＿＿＿＿＿＿＿

7. eyes are cold and remote. →   ＿＿＿＿＿＿＿＿＿＿＿＿＿

8. eyes are vicious.   →   ＿＿＿＿＿＿＿＿＿＿＿＿＿

二、翻譯

1. 氣質是裝不出來的，因為它是人重要的一部分。

A p＿＿＿＿＿ t＿＿＿＿＿ and d＿＿＿＿＿ is an e＿＿＿＿＿

p＿＿＿＿＿ of his c＿＿＿＿＿.

三、Crossword Puzzles

請將以下所提示的英文單字填入字謎：

1. 劍 (s...d)，子彈 (b...t)，虛偽的 (h...l)，哲學 (p...y)，圓熟的 (m...w)

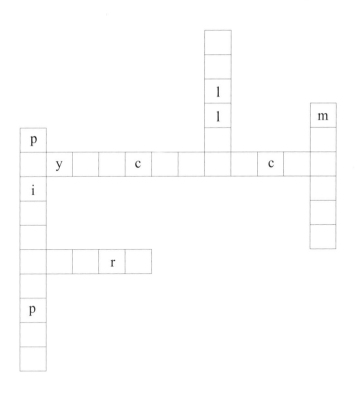

2. 有效率的 (e...t)，節拍 (t...o)，同伴 (c...n)，冷漠的 (r...e)，曖昧不明的
   (a...s)

答案

一、填充

1. peaceful heart

2. cheerful heart

3. self-fulfillment

4. slow breathing

6. They may not be sincere.

7. They may not be willing to share.

8. They may take away your peace of mind.

二、翻譯

1. person's temperament, disposition, essential part, character

三、Crossword Puzzles

1. **Across** hypocritical, sword

   Down philosophy, bullet, mellow

2. **Across** efficient, remote, ambiguous

   Down tempo, companion

22 錢用對了地方，才有價值

在無人的沙漠中，一袋黃金不如一瓶水，而且黃金還可能是重擔。

在愛情中，名車不如摩托車，而且名車可能招來虛情假意。

所以，錢要用在適當的地方，發揮它最大的效用，才能展現它的價值。

我們都誇大了金錢的重要性。金錢沒有固定的價值，它可以輕如鵝毛，也可以決定生死。它唯一不變的奇蹟在於「愈給愈有」：我們寬待他人，人生必善待我們。

Words of Wisdom

A miser's money takes the place of wisdom.
　　小氣鬼
➡ 意指：人一小氣，就會心胸狹隘，當然就失掉了智慧。

Money Isn't Everything

· ·

Money is an important part of life, and one should learn to manage it wisely, but it isn't everything.

In a barren[1] desert,[2] a bottle of water is more valuable than a bag of gold, which is actually a burden because of its weight.

On a date, a scooter[3] can be more valuable than a BMW because a girl holding tightly to her date on the back of a scooter can have a closer bonding experience than a girl sitting in the passenger seat of a car.[*]

The necessity of money has been greatly exaggerated. The value of money depends on the situation. It can be totally useless in one case and incomparably[4] influential[5] in another. The only unchangeable truth is that its utility[6] increases when we share it—life is generous to us when we are generous to others.

★ 因爲文化不同，不適合完全照中文翻譯出來

重要字彙

① barren [ˈbærən] (adj.) 不育的；荒蕪的
② desert [ˈdɛzət] (n.) 沙漠
　【比較】dessert [dɪˈzɜt] (n.) 甜點（記憶方法：甜點愈多愈好，所以有兩個 "s"）
③ scooter [ˈskutə] (n.) 摩托車
　motorcycle [ˈmotəˌsaɪkl] (n.) 重型機車
④ incomparable [ɪnˈkɑmpərəbl] (adj.) 無人能比的
⑤ influential [ˌɪnfluˈɛnʃəl] (adj.) 有影響的
⑥ utility [juˈtɪlətɪ] (n.) 用處

UNIT 23　錢的奴才

‧‧

不管有錢或沒錢，如果我們太容易被金錢掌控，就成了它的奴才：

　——當我們有錢的時候，如果盛氣凌人，就失掉了尊嚴。

　——當我們沒有錢的時候，如果唉聲嘆氣，就失掉了快樂。

　——當我們看到有錢人，如果心生羨慕，就失掉了平靜。

　——當我們面對有錢人，如果低聲下氣，就失掉了瀟灑自在。

如果我們是這樣的人，不管口袋有沒有錢，心靈都很窮，經常受錢的罪，情緒不得釋放，是百分之百的奴僕。

Words of Wisdom

Contentment is worth more than riches.

財富

Are We Slaves to Money?

. . . .

Rich or poor, if we are controlled by money, we are its slave.

■ If we are scornful[1] when we are rich, we have lost perspective.[2]

■ If we are depressed when we are poor, we have lost happiness.

■ If we are jealous when we see rich people, we have lost our peace of mind.

■ If we are petty[3] when we are with rich people, we have lost our humanity.[4]

All the money in the world does not mean a thing if you are lacking in spirit, compassion,[5] or character. One whose life is ruled by money has been deprived of his or her freedom and soul.

重要字彙

① scornful [ˈskɔrnfəl] (adj.) 很賤的
② perspective [pɚˈspɛktɪv] (n.) 層次、深邃之處
③ petty [ˈpɛtɪ] (adj.) 渺小的
④ humanity [hjuˈmænətɪ] (n.) 人性
⑤ compassion [kəmˈpæʃən] (n.) 同情心

錢的主人

其實，只要心態對了，不管有錢沒錢，我們都可以成為錢的主人：

當我們沒錢的時候──事出必有因，自我反省。

當我們看到有錢人的時候──見賢思齊，給自己一個樂觀的動力。

當我們面對有錢人的時候──心如止水，自由自在，你過你的日子，我過我的日子。

當我們有錢的時候──簡樸過日、樂於助人，因為授人玫瑰，手留餘香。

窮人節儉，出於無奈；富人節儉，真是瀟灑。

Words of Wisdom

Win your lawsuit and love your money.
　　　　　　訴訟
➡ 意指：當然想打贏官司，但別忘了訴訟要花錢！ 意指：錢要用對地方。

84

Become the Master of Money

· ·

We can all become masters of money if we put ourselves in the right frame of mind.

When we are poor, we can ask ourselves, "Why?" There must be a reason.

When we see the rich, we should become inspired:[1] What can we learn from them?

When we are with the rich, our hearts should be at peace. Be happy for them, and be thankful for your own blessings.

When we are rich, a frugal[2] yet generous life is the true sign of good character.

Some pinch pennies[3] because they have to, but a wealthy person who wastes nothing and lives a frugal life is truly someone to be admired.

重要字彙

① inspire [ɪnˋspaɪr] (v.) 激勵
② frugal [ˋfrugl̩] (adj.) 節省的
③ pinch pennies [pɪntʃ ˋpɛnɪz] (v.) 省錢、錙銖必較

我為什麼沒錢？

貧窮通常是有原因的。

——如果學歷不夠，想一想：年少時，當別人在用功讀書的時候，我也一樣用功、或者學習一技之長嗎？

——如果失業，想一想：當我有工作機會時，我比別人更認真嗎？

——如果貧困，想一想：當我曾有若干金錢時，有沒有簡樸過日，未雨綢繆？有沒有更積極而審慎地理財呢？

——如果因為身體不適而無法工作，因而失業，想一想，當別人運動、養生時，我也努力維持健康嗎？

高學歷不一定使我們致富，萬貫家財也不能保證我們一生富貴。**態度才能決定口袋。**

（本文不一定適合每個人，若有些嚴苛之處，尚請讀者見諒。）

Words of Wisdom

Rich men accumulate money; the poor accumulate years.

累積

Why Am I Poor?

Oftentimes, there is a reason why someone is poor. While some of these reasons may sound cruel, many illustrate[1] facts that should be reflected on.[2]

How does your diploma or grades compare to those of your competitors?[3] If they are inferior,[4] what were you doing at school while others were studying?

If you got laid off, was it because you did not work as hard as other people?

If you have no savings, is it because you did not lead a frugal life? Did you save properly and manage your money wisely?

If you lost your job due to poor health, did you try to maintain a healthy lifestyle while others were eating healthily and exercising?

Neither a good education nor a large inheritance[5] can guarantee lifelong wealth. Your attitude and money management skills will ultimately[6] decide what is in your bank account.

重要字彙

① illustrate [ˋɪləstret] (v.) 圖解；說明
② reflect on [rɪˋflɛkt ɑn] (n.) 反省
③ competitor [kəmˋpɛtətə] (n.) 競爭者
④ inferior [ɪnˋfɪrɪə] (adj.) 較差
⑤ inheritance [ɪnˌhɛrɪtəns] (n.) 繼承財產；遺產
⑥ ultimately [ˋʌltəmɪtlɪ] (adv.) 最終

Exercise

一、填充

1. If we are scornful when we are rich,

   → We have lost our _____.

2. If we are depressed when we are poor,

   → We have lost _____.

3. If we are jealous when we see rich people,

   → We have lost our _____ of _____.

4. If we feel petty when we are with rich people,

   → We have lost our _____.

二、翻譯

1. 我該反省一下。

   I should _____ _____ myself.

2. 我的形象比他差。

   My _____ is _____ _____ his.

3. 一個節省的人和小氣的人是不一樣的。

   A _____ person is _____ from a _____ one.

三、Crossword Puzzles

請將以下所提示的英文單字填入字謎：

1. 荒蕪的 (b...n)，沙漠 (d...t)，甜點 (d...t)，摩托車 (s...r)，有影響的 (i...l)，欺騙 (d...e)，用圖說明 (i...e)

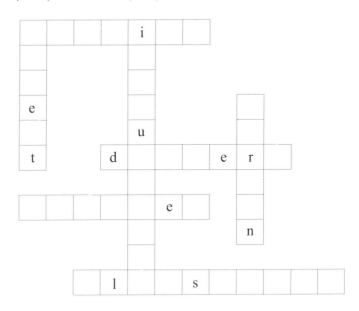

2. 渺小的 (p...y)，人性 (h...y)，同情心 (c...n)，層次或深度 (p...e)，節省的 (f...l)，遺產 (i...e)

答案

一、填充

1. perspective
2. happiness
3. peace, mind
4. humanity

二、翻譯

1. reflect on
2. image, inferior to
3. frugal, different, stingy

三、Crossword Puzzles

1. **Across** deceive, dessert, scooter, illustrate

   Down desert, influential, barren
2. **Across** perspective, humanity

   Down compassion, frugal, petty, inheritance

Notes . . .

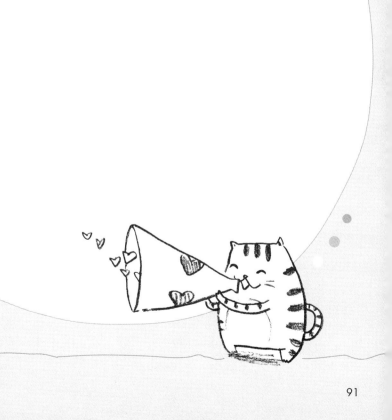

UNIT 26 富人與窮人

有些窮人很富裕，有些富人卻很貧窮：

——窮人沒有錢，只能吃粗茶淡飯、常做勞力的工作，結果身體更健康。

——窮人穿 199 元的衣服、100 元的鞋子、穿得美美的、十分滿意。

——富人錢多多，常吃美食，文明病隨之而來。

——富人的市場永遠有更貴的衣服、有更美的鞋子，令人趨之若鶩、暗中較勁、永不知足。

誰是窮人？誰是富人？我不知道，因為，**財富並非決定貧富的絕對條件**！

Words of Wisdom

Fools live poor to die rich.

➡ 意指：許多人一輩子捨不得用錢，死了以後，留下一堆錢。這是不智的行為。John D.Rockefeller 勸人捐贈的一句話可呼應：It's a shame to die rich.。

Rich People and Poor People

. . . .

Poor people often eat simple food and work with their hands or perform manual[1] labor, which keeps them in good health.

Affordable clothes can look and feel just as good as overpriced expensive ones.

Rich people often sit at desks long hours, eat at expensive restaurants, and indulge[2] in rich delicacies.[3]

More expensive clothes and shoes always await those who are not satisfied and love to compete.[4]

Are the rich really rich? Are the poor really poor? If you think of wealth in terms of health or happiness, who is rich and who is poor is not determined by money.

重要字彙

① manual [ˈmænjʊəl] (adj.) 手工的
② indulge [ɪnˈdʌldʒ] (v.) 放縱
③ delicacy [ˈdɛləkəsɪ] (n.) 精美
④ compete [kəmˈpit] (v.) 比賽、競爭
　 competitor [kəmˈpɛtətə] (n.) 競爭者

誰娶了賢妻？

我們常見到這樣的現象：

一個富家子，娶了一個女孩。這位妻子每天睡到自然醒、打扮漂亮，喝茶逛街。丈夫有所挫敗時，她無能為力。丈夫失敗時，她離他而去。

一個貧家子，也娶了一個女孩。這位妻子每天早起、辛苦持家、外出工作，和丈夫一同分擔家計。丈夫有所挫敗，她相伴相隨。

他們哪一位娶了賢妻？錢在他們的婚姻中扮演了什麼角色？

Words of Wisdom

Much money, much love.

Money and Marriage

· ·

Many people envy a rich man who marries a beautiful and fashionable[1] woman. But while he is working, she is shopping. When he is stressed or frustrated,[2] he suffers alone. And if his career falters,[3] she may be out the door.

Not many people think about the poor man who marries a practical woman who works hard to help sustain[4] the home and shares in all the family expenses. When he suffers, she is right there by his side.

Which man is luckier? Which man is truly richer?

重要字彙

① fashionable [ˈfæʃənəbl̩] (adj.) 時尚的
② frustration [ˌfrʌsˈtreʃən] (n.) 挫折
③ falter [ˈfɔltə] (v.) 在危難中、搖晃
④ sustain [səˈsten] (v.) 使持續下去

UNIT 28 不必羨慕富人的孩子

富人的兒女可以從小學鋼琴、學畫畫、學跳舞。

富人的兒女可以吃好的、穿好的。

富人的兒女從小到大都沒有金錢的壓力。

富人的兒女所聽到的話都是友善、誇讚、奉承。

不過，富人的兒女從小要什麼有什麼，再也沒什麼東西可以引起他們拍手欣喜。

富人的兒女進入社會時，超低的抗壓性讓他們容易受傷。

富人的兒女不深知辛勤工作或犧牲的意義。

可以說，他們可能被父母的財富犧牲了。

所以，窮人的孩子別氣餒，從另一個角度來說，你也是有福的。

Words of Wisdom

子宮

For rich and poor the womb is equally warm.

➡ 意指：我們應平等對待窮人和富人。

Rich Parents and Strawberry Children

· ·

There are many advantages to having rich parents:

— piano lessons, dance classes, or art instructors from a young age;

— a big house in a nice neighborhood, expensive clothes, and fancy food;

— no financial pressure.

But there are also disadvantages:

— You are not easy to satisfy because you are used to nice things.

— Having been sheltered[1] your whole life, you may be vulnerable[2] when you step into the real world.

— You never learn the meaning of hard work or sacrifice.

★

   It can be nice to have rich parents, but there are also many reasons to be thankful if yours are not.

★ 英文部分不適合譯出他們被父母的財富犧牲了，因爲西方人的孩子一般較爲獨立。

重要字彙

① shelter [ˈʃɛltə] (v.)(n.) 蔽護；遮蓋物
② vulnerable [ˈvʌlnərəbl] (adj.) 易受傷的

一、填充

1. Advantages to having rich parents（有富爸爸，就常有以下）：

鋼琴課	舞蹈課	藝術課

p_____l_____   d_____c_____   a_____i_____

好區的大房子   昂貴的衣服

a b_____h_____in a n_____n_____   e_____c_____

時尚美食   沒有金錢壓力

f_____f_____n_____   f_____p_____

2. Disadvantages to having rich parents（有富爸爸，也常有以下）：

不易知足   抗壓力差

n_____e_____s_____   v_____

不懂辛勤和犧牲的意義

n_____a_____of h_____w_____or s_____

二、Crossword Puzzles

請將以下所提示的英文單字填入字謎：

1. 手工的 (m...l)，放縱 (i...e)，

    精細 (d...y)，競爭者 (c...r)

2. 時尚的 (f...e)，挫折 (f...n)，在危難中 (f...r)，持續 (s...n)，甩掉 (d...p)，背叛 (b...y)

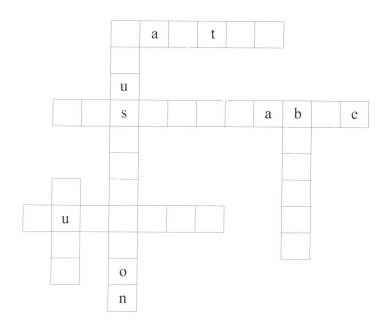

 答案

一、填充

1. piano lessons, dance classes, art instructions, a big house in a nice neighborhood, expensive clothes, fancy food, no financial pressure
2. not easily satisfied, vulnerable, not aware of hard work or sacrifice

二、**Crossword Puzzles**

1. **Across** manual, delicacy
   Down competitor, indulge
2. **Across** falter, fashionable, sustain
   Down dump, frustration, betray

做生命的畫家

水放著不喝，擺了沒用。

車擺著不開，買了沒用。

浪費生命，等於白活。

生命就像一本空白的畫紙，一人一本，不多不少。每個人也都是生命的畫家。生命最大的意義不在於我們得到多少，而是能建構多少。

每一個人對自己的生命畫冊負責，當我們到晚年時，把這本畫冊打開，看看自己在裡面畫了些什麼？

Words of Wisdom

Every day of your life is a page of your history.

The Canvas of Life

Water is wasted unless it's used.

A car is wasted unless it's driven.

An unproductive[1] life is no life at all.

We all have just one canvas[2]—no more, no less. We can fill our canvas with things like good deeds, wonderful experiences, and good times with family. We can also waste the canvas with negativity[3] or by doing nothing at all. In the end, the most valuable canvas will be the painting that we look back on with delight.[4]

In your old age, when you reflect on the canvas of your life, what will you see?

重要字彙

① unproductive [ˌʌnprəˋdʌktɪv] (adj.) 沒建設的、沒貢獻的
② canvas [ˋkænvəs] (n.) 帆布、畫布
③ negativity [ˌnɛgəˋtɪvətɪ] (n.) 負面事情
④ delight [dɪˋlaɪt] (n.) (v.) 欣喜

日日是好日

一年三百六十五天，每天都是一個新的旅程，沒人知道它將出現什麼好事情，也可能失掉誰，但是我們每天都要勇敢喜樂地踏上這個旅程。

最了不起的人是，無論日子有多苦，心中的笑臉沒人能拿得走！

過一日如過一世，天天都要把它過地最好！快樂的生活是由快樂的想法組成的。快樂一天，就賺到一天！

Words of Wisdom

A wise man's day is worth a fool's life.

Every Day Is a Good Day

. . . .

Every single day can be looked at as a new journey. Anything can happen on any day. A bit of good fortune may cross your path, or someone important to you might disappear from your life. But you should always step into every new day with courage and happiness.

The most remarkable[1] person is the one who can smile even through the tough[2] times.

When you consider that your whole life is simply made up of many individual days, it is easy to see why you would want to make every day a happy one. If you have felt happy for a day, not only have you won that day, but you have also taken one step toward having an exceedingly[3] happy life.

重要字彙

① remarkable [rɪˋmɑrkəbl] (*adj.*) 非凡的
② tough [tʌf] (*adj.*) 堅韌的
③ exceedingly [ɪkˋsidɪŋlɪ] (*adv.*) 極度地

一個傑作

　　我認識一個女孩子，高中畢業之後父母就不准她上學，她開始養家。

　　從此，這對年僅四十歲左右的父母不再工作，而這女孩早上四點就去早餐店幫忙洗菜、整理食物；中午十一點再到游泳池賣票，一直做到晚上十一點下班，日日如此。

　　現在她二十五歲了，工作依舊，而且下了班還要去醫院照顧因吸毒而洗腎的父親。

　　她生命的意義在哪裏？**她生命的意義在於她決心要好好地畫這一張生命的畫作：**

A Masterpiece¹ of a Person

• •

I know a young woman whose parents forbade her to go to school after high school.

When she graduated, her parents, who were in their 40s, quit their jobs. Instead of working themselves, they put their daughter to work. At 4:00 a.m. she would clock in at a breakfast place to wash vegetables and cook. After her shift,² she would rush to a swimming pool where she sold tickets and got off at 11:00 p.m.

She is now 25 years old and still works at the breakfast shop and pool. But these days instead of going home at 11:00 p.m., she goes to the hospital to take care of her father, who is in bad health.

It may be easy to wonder, "What hope can she have?" However, she has become determined to fill the canvas of her life with great art.

重要字彙

① masterpiece [ˈmæstəˌpis] (n.) 傑作
② shift [ʃɪft] (n.) (v.) 輪班

——我常拿書給她看，她不斷地閱讀，所以不但有豐沛的知識，而且氣質很好。

——她樂於助人，所以人緣很好。

——她太忙了，所以只要偶爾放一天假，就可以讓她滿心期待，藏不住滿臉的笑意。

因為她肯吃苦、氣質好、人緣好、樂觀、自信、又能幹，所以游泳池的幾個會員都搶著把自己條件不錯的兒子介紹給她。她比誰都有資格終日自憐，但是她決定做生命的操盤手。

Words of Wisdom

Life is partly what we make it and partly what it is made by the friends we choose.

She wants to learn and improve as a person, so I often bring books for her to read. She likes to help people—a trait that has earned her many great friends. She is so busy that even one day of freedom can bring her indescribable[3] joy.

Because she is frugal, hard working, well-poised,[4] pleasant, confident, and capable, almost all the parents who swim at the pool want to introduce her to their sons. This young woman could hardly be blamed for indulging[5] in self-pity, but instead she has chosen to become a winner in life.

重要字彙

③ indescribable [ˌɪndɪˈskraɪbəbl] (*adj.*) 難以描述的
④ well-poised [ˈwɛlˈpɔɪzd] (*adj.*) 舉止得宜的
⑤ indulge [ɪnˈdʌldʒ] (*v.*) 縱容

一、翻譯

1. 我們的一生是由許許多多的「一天」所譜成。

   Our e_____ life is m_____ u_____ o_____

   many i_____ d_____.

2. 每天都有可能發生任何事。

   A_____ can h_____ on a_____ day.

3. 最棒的人是無論日子多苦,都能微笑以對!

   The m_____ r_____ p_____ is the o_____ who

   s_____ even th_____ the t_____ t_____.

二、Crossword Puzzles

請將以下所提示的英文單字
填入字謎:

1. 帆布 (c...s),
   不具生產力的 (u...e),
   負面的事 (n...y),
   庇護 (s...r),
   脆弱的 (v...e)

n	e				i		
o							
		s		l			
v	u			r			

2. 大作 (m...e)，旅程 (j...y)，堅韌的 (t...h)，過度極度地 (e...y)，了不起的 (r...e)，欣喜 (d...t)

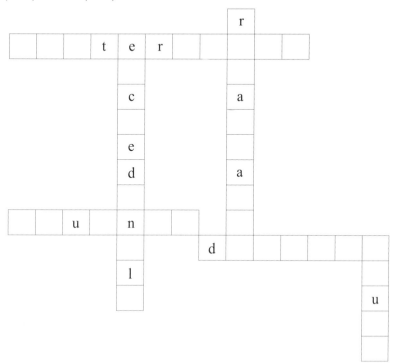

 答案

一、翻譯

1. entire, made up of, individual days

2. Anything, happen, any

3. most, remarkable person, one, smiles, through, tough times

二、**Crossword Puzzles**

1. `Across` negativity, shelter, vulnerable

   `Down` unproductive, canvas

2. `Across` masterpiece, journey, delight

   `Down` exceedingly, remarkable, tough

我們也可成為藝術品

舒適的穿著——讓我們感覺自在。

健康的頭髮——讓我們看起來有精神。

乾淨的皮膚——讓我們看起來潔淨。

優雅的儀態——讓我們吸引人。

安靜的眼神——讓我們安撫緊張。

認真地工作——讓我們受人尊重。

溫柔的聲音——讓我們聽來溫暖。

善良的心——讓我們融化仇恨和敵對。

甜甜的微笑——讓我們賞心悅目。

我們也可以成為藝術品。

Words of Wisdom

本質　　　　　　　　　　　　　感恩
The essence of all beautiful art is gratitude.
➡ 意指：沒有一顆感恩的心，就沒有愉悅寧靜的情懷。少了這種情懷，哪還有美？

You Too Can Be a Masterpiece!

· ·

Wearing comfortable clothes makes you feel at ease.

Healthy hair makes you look fresh.

★

Elegant posture is attractive.

If you are calm, others will follow suit.[1]

Hard work earns respect.

A soft voice exudes[2] warmth.

A kind heart dissolves[3] hatred[4] and hostility.[5]

A sweet smile makes everyone feel good.

You too can be a masterpiece!

★ 在西方因為種族問題敏感，所以「膚色」在此不宜譯出。

重要字彙

① follow suit (v.) 模仿
② exude [ɪgˋzjud] (v.) 散發
③ dissolve [dɪˋzɑlv] (v.) 融解
④ hatred [ˋhetrɪd] (n.) 憎恨
⑤ hostility [hɑsˋtɪlətɪ] (n.) 敵意

每一個藝術作品都是心血,它傳遞了藝術工作者內心的感動。

——藝人在街頭畫畫,我們不妨靜靜地觀賞。

——藝人在街頭演奏,我們也可以停下腳步,認真聆聽。

——欣賞之後,奉上若干金錢,感謝他們努力和我們分享。

和街頭藝人邂逅,是一項同時「施」與「受」的美事。不要對自己吝嗇,也不要對他們小氣。

Words of Wisdom

He who has an art has everywhere a part.

➡ 解釋:心中有藝術的人,到任何地方,都有其重要性。

Appreciate Street Artists

· ·

All art is precious because it comes from the soul of the artist.

Stop and try to appreciate the work of a street artist when you encounter[1] one. Don't be stingy if you feel that you gain something positive[2] from it. Give the artist some encouragement and a donation,[3] and thank him or her for sharing the art.

Appreciating a street artist is a wonderful give-and-take experience.

重要字彙

① encounter [ɪn`kaʊntə] (v.)(n.) 偶然相遇
② positive [`pazətɪv] (adj.) 確定的
③ donation [do`neʃən] (n.) 捐獻

最美的畫作

世界上最好的畫作，就是大自然。

黎明的晨光、黃昏的晚霞；

挺拔的大樹、柔軟的小草；

奔騰的海浪、潺潺的小溪；

金亮的陽光、迷濛的薄霧；

鮮紅的蘋果、嫩綠的青棗……

再偉大的畫家，也就不過把大自然逼真地呈現出來而已。

原作就在眼前，我們看到了嗎？

Words of Wisdom

Art imitates nature.

The Most Beautiful Works of Art

• •

The greatest works of art can be found in nature.

Twilight[1] and sunset glow.[2]

Tall strong trunks and slender grass.

Galloping[3] sea waves and running creeks.[4]

Glowing sun beams and translucent[5] mists.

Rose red apples and jadeite[6] green dates.[7]

The greatest artists only hope to display an authentic[8] representation of nature.

The prototype[9] for all art is right before your eyes—have you seen it?

重要字彙

① twilight [ˈtwaɪˌlaɪt] (n.) 黎明之光
② sunset glow (n.) 晚霞
③ gallop [ˈgæləp] (v.) 奔馳
④ creek [ˈkrik] (n.) 小溪
⑤ translucent [trænsˈlusn̩t] (adj.) 半透明的

⑥ jadeite [ˈdʒedaɪt] (n.) 翡翠
⑦ date [det] (n.) 棗子
⑧ authentic [ɔˈθɛntɪk] (adj.) 逼真的
⑨ prototype [ˈprotəˌtaɪp] (n.) 原版

雨是好東西

不要討厭下雨，因為它是一個好東西。

雨水替花草、大地、房屋行洗禮，如果不下雨，豈不是到處又髒又臭？

雨珠也是寶。撐著傘出去走一走，看看掛在欄杆上的小雨珠，各個晶瑩剔透，就像一顆顆小水晶球；我們再貼近看看，它表面的世界都是乾乾淨淨，而且你知道嗎？水珠裏面的世界上下顛倒呢！有趣極了！

下雨了嗎？走出去吧！**打開心眼，張開肉眼**，走入大自然的洗禮吧！不然，在窗邊看著風景、看本好書，也很享受呢！

Words of Wisdom

Art has no enemy but ignorance.

➡ 意指：藝術唯一的敵人，就是「無知」，即「無知之人不喜藝術」。

Welcome the Rain

It is easy to get annoyed[1] on a rainy day, but where would we be without rain?

Rain nourishes[2] flowers, grass, and trees. It gives life. It also cleans streets, houses, and buildings.

Raindrops are like gemstones.[3] Take a walk in the rain and look closely at the drops hanging off rails[4] and fences.[5] Each one is like a tiny crystal ball in which the world is turned upside down![6]

Instead of complaining about a rainy day, enjoy it! Go out and cool yourself with a refreshing natural shower, or curl[7] up next to a window with a good book and enjoy the scene.

重要字彙

① annoyed [ə`nɔɪd] (adj.) 被煩的
② nourish [`nɝɪʃ] (v.) 滋養
③ gemstone [`dʒɛm͵ston] (n.) 寶石
④ rail [rel] (n.) 欄杆

⑤ fence [fɛns] (n.) 籬笆；圍牆
⑥ upside down 上下顛倒的
⑦ curl [kɝl] (v.) 捲曲著

一、填充

A. 試著讓自己成為藝術品：

1. Comfortable clothes → *make you feel at ease*

2. Healthy hair →

3. Elegant posture →

4. A calm look →

5. Hard work →

6. A soft voice →

7. A kind heart →

8. A sweet smile →

B. 請填入英文

1. 美麗的陽光：_____ and _____
　　　　　　　　　晨光　　　　　　　　晚霞

2. 展現生命的樹：_____ and _____
　　　　　　　　　大樹幹　　　　　　　細草

3. 流動的水：_____ and _____
　　　　　　　奔騰的海浪　　　　　　潺潺的流水

4. 顏色誘人的水果：_____ and _____
　　　　　　　　　紅若玫瑰的蘋果　　　翠綠的棗子

C. Rain is good stuff.

1.   Rain

   nourishes

2.   Rain

                                                                       cleans

3.   Rain

                gives

4. Each raindrop

   is like

二、Crossword Puzzle

請將以下所提示的英文單字填入字謎：

1. 邂逅 (e...r)，樂觀正面的 (p...e)，捐獻 *n.* (d...n)，恨 *n.* (h...d)，敵意 (h...y)，融解 (d...e)

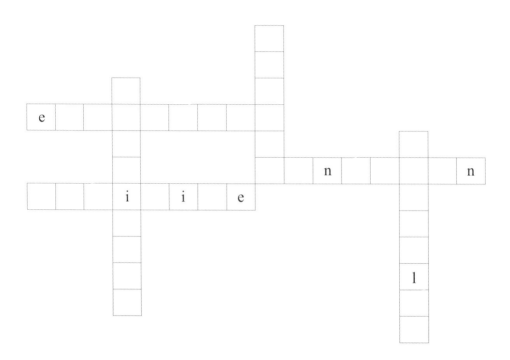

答案

一、填充

A.

2. makes you look fresh

3. is attractive

4. makes others follow suit

5. earns respect

6. exudes warmth

7. dissolves hatred and hostility

8. makes everyone feel good

B.

1. twilight, sunset glow

2. tall strong trunks, slender grass

3. galloping sea waves, running creeks

4. rose red apples, jadeite green dates

C.

1. flowers, grass, trees

2. streets, houses, buildings

3. life

4. a gemstone/a tiny crystal ball

二、**Crossword Puzzle**

Across encounter, donation, positive

Down hostility, hatred, dissolve

UNIT 36 死亡是生命的一部分

生命就是一趟旅行，這一輛生命列車上的每一個人，都會下車。

有些人在台北上車，在板橋就下車了；有些人在新竹上車，在台中下車；也有一些人則一路搭到高雄，最後仍然必須下車。

搭過火車的人都知道，每一站都有人上，每一站也都有人下，沒什麼大不了的！生命列車和火車唯一不同的是，我們自己不能決定在哪一站下車。正因為如此，更要好好地把握車上的時光，看看風景、看看書、吃吃便當、聊聊天、交交朋友，享受這只能坐一趟的生命列車。

該下車了？心懷感恩、高高興興地下車吧。最怕的是死抓著車門不放──**最終都得下去，何必走得那麼難看呢？**

Words of Wisdom

Death is but death. All in time shall die.

Dying Is a Part of Life

. . . .

Life is like a train. Everyone has to get off eventually.[1]

For some, the journey is short. Some people get on the train at Taipei station and get off at Banqiao. Others get on at Hsinchu and get off at Taichung. Some people do not get off until Kaohsiung—a long journey indeed. But they will still leave the train eventually.

All those who have taken a train know that at every station there are people getting on and people getting off. It's a familiar pattern.[2] Life works the same way. The only difference is that we can't always choose where we would like to get off. Because we don't know how long we'll be on the train, we should appreciate every minute: enjoy the scenery, do some reading, have a meal, chat[3] with your companions, or make a new friend. Make the most of it whatever you do because you only have one trip!

Time to leave the train? Get off with a grateful heart! Never grab the door and refuse to go—that's a fight that no one can win. The best you can do is to leave with grace and dignity.[4]

重要字彙

① eventually [ɪˋvɛntʃʊəlɪ] (adv.) 終究
② pattern [ˋpætən] (n.) 模式
③ chat [tʃæt] (v.) 聊天
④ dignity [ˋdɪgnətɪ] (n.) 莊嚴

瀟灑看待生離死別

先父是一位幽默、善良、感情豐富、非常天真的學者,也是一等一的好爸爸。或許因為我長得和他十分相像,他一直最疼愛我,到哪裡都必定帶著我。但是,從父親過世至今五年,我雖日日思念那深切而溫柔的父愛,卻幾乎未曾流淚。

人說:「生離死別是人生之最苦。」其實,緣起緣滅、一切順勢而為,不必牽強。

所愛的人要下車了,感謝他一路相伴,並輕輕地揮手向他道別。

Words of Wisdom

Death is not the greatest loss in life. The greatest loss is what dies inside us while we live.

Instead of Mourning a Departure, Celebrate a Life!

$\bullet$ $\bullet$

My late father was a humorous, kind, loving, even child-like scholar and one of the best dads in the world.

I was the favorite of his six children probably because I resembled[1] him the most. I think of him day and night but haven't shed[2] many tears since he passed away five years ago. Departures[3] are painful, but they are an unavoidable[4] part of life.

Instead of being depressed about or mourning[5] a loved one who is leaving the train, celebrate his or her life! Thank them for their companionship[6] and contribution, and wave them off into the sunset.

重要字彙

① resemble [rɪˋzɛmbl̩] (v.) 類似
② shed [ʃɛd] (v.) 流下
③ departure [dɪˋpartʃə] (n.) 離開
④ unavoidable [ˌʌnəˋvɔɪdəbl̩] (adj.) 不可避免的
⑤ mourn [morn] (v.) 哀悼
⑥ companionship [kəmˋpænjənˌʃɪp] (n.) 友誼、陪伴

125

拿掉了恐懼，死亡還剩什麼？

　　死亡最大的權勢，就是恐懼。其實，死亡也是生命的一部分，神當年把我們順利地帶到這世上，以後必也會順利地把我們帶走。

　　正如聖經上的一句話：「神的恩典是夠我們用的。」我們的日子如何，力量也必如何，不必畏懼死亡。**在這天天都有人離去的世界，我們活著的每一天，都是恩典**，要歡喜快樂地把它過地最好。

　　星雲大師說得好：「**活也好，死也好，都好。**」

Words of Wisdom

Death and tax are both certain, but death isn't annual.

一年一次

Don't Be Afraid of Death

The greatest power that death has over us is fear, but death is as much a part of our reality as life. As easily as we have been put onto this world, we can just as easily be taken away.

The Bible says, "My grace is sufficient for you." Do not be afraid of death. Be grateful for life and make the most of the time you have.

After fear is removed, death has no hold over us.

一、填充

1. The greatest power that death has over us is

2. Death is a part of

3.   for life

4. Make the most of

二、Crossword Puzzles

請將以下所提示的英文單字填入字謎：

1. 最終 (e...y)，型式 (p...n)，聊天 (c...t)，被弄煩的 (a...d)，寶石 (g...e)，
   雨滴 (r...p)，欄杆 (r...l)

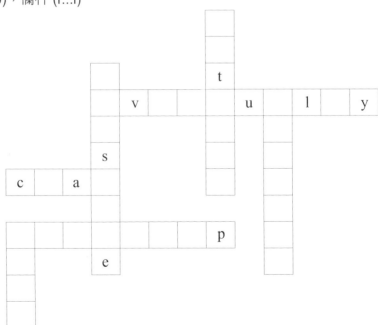

2. 相像 (r...e)，「流」淚 (s...d)，不可避免的 (u...e)，離別 (d...e)，呻吟 (m...n)，陪伴 (c...p)，操守 (d...y)

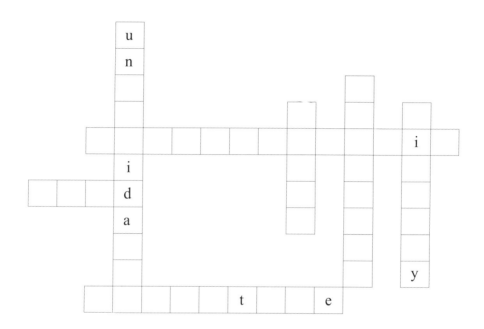

 答案

一、填充

1. fear
2. life

3. Be grateful
4. the time we have

二、**Crossword Puzzles**

1. Across eventually, chat, raindrop

   Down rail, gemstone, pattern, annoyed

2. Across companionship, shed, departure

   Down unavoidable, mourn, resemble, dignity

傻瓜才被激怒

「急躁」輕易地暴露我們的弱點,並損毀我們的形象。急躁也傷肝傷脾,更使我們的心靈失去平衡。在任何情況下,我們一開始急躁,就輸了:

——有人罵我們笨的像豬,我們何妨一笑置之?反正我們不是豬!

——在馬路上開車,不必去爭那口氣,因為就算爭贏了,也沒有獎品。

Control Your Emotions

• •

Those whose temperament[1] is easily affected by others have a significant weakness. If you are easily irritated[2] or angered over trivial things,[3] you will experience high amounts of stress and lack control of your life. According to Chinese medicine, such things are bad for the liver[4] and spleen.[5]

If someone calls you an idiot,[6] the best thing you can do is to ignore them—after all, you are not an idiot.

It is pointless[7] to get into arguments on the road because nothing is ever accomplished by doing this. In situations like these, there are no winners.

> **重要字彙**

① temperament [ˈtɛmprəmənt] (*n.*) 性情
② irritate [ˈɪrəˌtet] (*v.*) 激怒
③ trivial thing [ˈtrɪvɪəl θɪŋ] 小事
④ liver [ˈlɪvə] (*n.*) 肝
⑤ spleen [splin] (*n.*) 脾
⑥ idiot [ˈɪdɪət] (*n.*) 白痴
⑦ pointless [ˈpɔɪntlɪs] (*adj.*) 沒意義的

試試看，我們是否可以永遠不被人激怒？因為常被激怒的人，就像小木偶，隨著別人手中牽的線而左右擺動。面對惡意批評而心仍靜如水的人，真酷！

　　在順勢中愉快，不算什麼，只有時時刻刻保持平衡而愉快的人，才是一等一的高手！

　　何況，平心靜氣可長壽！

Words of Wisdom

He who angers you enslaves you.
　　　　主詞　　　　　　　奴役

Those who are easily provoked are like puppets controlled by those who provoke them. Being totally immune[8] to unconstructive[9] criticism[10] is really cool.

One who smiles during good times is nothing special. One who can smile through bad times has truly achieved something.

Having a calm mind with a peaceful heart is the recipe[11] for a long life.

重要字彙

[8] immune [ɪˋmjun] (*adj.*) 免疫的
[9] unconstructive [ˌʌnkənˋstrʌktɪv] (*adj.*) 沒建設性的
[10] criticism [ˋkrɪtəˌsɪzəm] (*n.*) 批評
[11] recipe [ˋrɛsəpɪ] (*n.*) 食譜

如老僧若定

我佩服出淤泥而不染的人，這種人有定見、有思想、有魄力！

許多人抽煙，一煙在手，好像很自在，其實被煙所捆綁，就失掉了「不抽煙」的自由。

許多人追隨流行，流行什麼就用什麼，看似走在時代的尖端，其實不過是商業行銷的應聲蟲。

許多人跟著別人一起吃搖頭丸，你一顆，我一顆，所謂「青春不留白，狂野一下無妨」——毒藥就是毒藥，它不會因為你是年輕人而失掉毒性。

冷靜一點，多想一下，你也可以成為出淤泥而不染的酷人。

Words of Wisdom

We must all suffer one of two things: the pain of discipline or the pain of regret.

自律

Be Your Own Person

••

I respect those who can be themselves under any circumstance.[1] These people are decisive,[2] insightful[3] and powerful.

Smokers think they're cool. In reality, they are weak-minded sheep who don't have the willpower[4] to break an addiction[5] that has been proven to be harmful.

Those who wear fashionable clothing think that everyone admires their sense of style. The truth is that they have actually over-paid to become walking commercial[6] propaganda.[7]

Youths who take ecstasy[8] are always partying and seem to be having a great time. The truth is that they have ingested[9] toxins[10] whose damage will remain long after youth has passed.

Always think before you act. Don't do anything that would keep you from being true to yourself.

> **重要字彙**

① circumstance [ˋsɝkəmˌstæns] (n.) 狀況、環境
② decisive [dɪˋsaɪsɪv] (adj.) 有魄力的
③ insightful [ˋɪnˌsaɪtfəl] (adj.) 有內涵的
④ willpower [ˋwɪlˌpaʊə] (n.) 魄力
⑤ addiction [əˋdɪkʃən] (n.) 上癮
⑥ commercial [kəˋmɝʃəl] (adj.) 商業的

⑦ propaganda [ˌprɑpəˋgændə] (n.) 宣傳
⑧ ecstasy [ˋɛkstəsɪ] (n.) 搖頭丸（原意是「極度歡愉」，簡稱 XTC）
⑨ ingest [ɪnˋdʒɛst] (v.) 攝取
⑩ toxin [ˋtɑksɪn] (n.) 毒

UNIT 41　生氣誤事

生氣時，不要教育兒女，以免言語傷人。

生氣時，不要開車，以免製造危險。

生氣時，不要談生意，以免判斷出錯。

生氣時，不要做任何決定，以免日後後悔。

生氣傷肝臟、傷心臟、傷脾臟，更使人面目醜陋。**氣死自己，親痛仇快，這聰明嗎**？

Words of Wisdom

The calmer you are, the further along you will go.

Anger Is Harmful

. . . .

To avoid verbal abuse, do not punish children in anger.

To avoid putting yourself or others in danger, do not drive in anger.

To avoid silly mistakes, do not negotiate[1] business in anger.

To avoid doing something you might regret, do not make any decisions in anger.

Anger harms the liver, heart, and spleen. Anger increases stress and clouds[2] judgment. Stay away from it!

重要字彙

① negotiate [nɪˋgoʃɪˏet] (v.) 談判
② cloud [klaud] (v.) 使……不好

忌妒催人老

這世上，有人比我們好，真是好事情！如果大家都比我們差，這世界也太慘了吧！**忌妒不會使自己更好，只會讓我們飽受煎熬，逐漸枯萎。**

這世界本來就由各式各樣的人組成：

別人比我們聰明——多一些聰明的人，社會就會更進步。
別人比我們可愛——多一些可愛的人，社會就會更愉悅。
別人比我們圓滑——多一些圓滑的人，社會就會更祥和。
別人比我們富裕——多一些富裕的人，總比多一些貧苦的人要好！
別人長的比我們好看——多一些好看的人，社會更賞心悅目。

幸福並不取決於財富、權利、成就、外貌。幸福來自於心境和胸懷，一個從不忌妒的胸懷更接近幸福。

Words of Wisdom

Jealousy has no holidays.

Jealousy Decays¹ the Bones

Jealousy only tortures² the soul with negativity. It does not make you better. Do not be jealous of the good fortune of others. The world would be a miserable place if no one were smarter, luckier, or more successful than you.

If people are smarter than us, be happy that they can keep the world progressing.

If people are better looking than us, be happy that they make the world more pleasant to look at.

If people are more diplomatic³ than us, be happy that they make the world more peaceful.

Your sense of self-worth should not come from comparisons. Instead, it should come from knowing that you are the best person that you can be.

重要字彙

① decay [dɪ`ke] (v.) 使腐敗
② torture [`tɔrtʃə] (v.)(n.) 折磨
③ diplomatic [ˌdɪplə`mætɪk] (adj.) 有外交手腕的

一、填充

A. Anger is harmful.

1. If we punish children in anger   →   *we might verbally abuse them.*

2. If we drive in anger   →

3. If we negotiate business in anger   →

4. If we make decisions in anger   →

B. Do not be jealous of the good fortunes of others, because···

1. If no one were smarter, luckier or more successful than us,

   →

2. If people are smarter than us,

   →

3. If people are better-looking than us,

   →

4. If people are more diplomatic than us,

   →

二、翻譯

1. 在馬路上和人爭執是沒意義的，因為什麼功能都沒有！

It's p_____ to g_____ i_____ a_____ on

the road because n_____ i_____ e_____

a_____.

2. 對沒有建設性的批評，我們如果可以完全不理會，就是真酷！

It's really c_____ ____ to be t_____ i_____ t_____

u_____ c_____.

3. 平心靜氣是長壽的祕訣！

A c_____ m_____ and a p_____ h_____ is

the r_____ f_____ a l_____ l_____.

4. 我尊敬那些出淤泥而不染的人。

I r_____ t_____ w_____ c_____ b_____

t_____ u_____ a_____ c_____.

5. 吸煙的人一點都不酷。

S_____ a_____ c_____ a_____

a_____.

6. 其實抽煙的人是脆弱的人，他們沒有堅定的意志力來脫離一個已被證實
會傷身體的惡習。

S_____ are w_____ -m_____ sh_____ who

d_____ h_____ t_____ w_____ to

b_____ an a_____ that has been p_____

t_____ b_____ h_____.

7. 搖頭丸的毒性會嚴重損傷我們的器官。

The t_____ of e_____ severely d_____ our

o_____.

8. 我們必須攝取足夠的鈣質。

We m_____ i_____ sufficient c_____.

 答案

一、填充

A.

2. we might put ourselves or others in danger.

3. we might make silly mistakes.

4. we might regret them.

B.

1. the world would be a miserable place.

2. they can keep the world progressing.

3. they make the world more pleasant to look at.

4. they make the world more peaceful.

二、翻譯

1. pointless, get into arguments, nothing is ever accomplished

2. cool, totally immune to unconstructive criticism

3. calm mind, peaceful heart, recipe for, long life

4. respect those who can be themselves under any circumstance

5. Smokers aren't cool at all

6. Smokers, weak-minded sheep, don't have the willpower, break, addiction, proven to be harmful

7. toxins, ecstasy, damage, organs

8. must ingest, calcium

Notes...

UNIT 43 穩著點兒！

我們恐懼的時候，心跳加快，呼吸急促——這是自虐！

我們恐懼的時候，心慌意亂，無法正常思考——難以成事！

我們恐懼的時候，信心全失、言語無味——全然暴露自己的弱點！

愈恐懼，要愈鎮定！

Words of Wisdom

Nothing in life is to be feared. It's only to be understood.

Stay Calm!

· ·

When we are frightened, our heart thumps,[1] our breath is short, we can't think clearly, and we lose confidence and speak improperly. That's why it's essential[2] to learn how to control our emotions[3] when we are in fear. The more frightening a situation is, the more essential it is to be calm and level-headed.[4]

重要字彙

① thump [θʌmp] (v.) 心跳加快
② essential [ɪ`sɛnʃəl] (adj.) 必要的
③ emotion [ɪ`moʃən] (n.) 情感
④ level-headed [`lɛvl`hɛdɪd] (adj.) 平穩的

最壞也不過如此

想一想，最壞的情況是什麼？

他離我而去？──不是我的，與其勉強留住，徒增痛苦，不如放彼此一條生路。

我失掉工作？──失掉工作是平常的，許多成功人士都曾失業。危機就是轉機，重整旗鼓，重新出發！

我罹患重病？──恐懼會使病情加重。面對它、處理它，若是未能治癒，就接受它，和它和平共處。

我怕東窗事發？──「誠實」和「勇敢」是不二法則。與其瞞了令人緊張，不如早點說開！

日子最壞大概也就如此！害怕也得過，勇敢也得過，我們要怎麼過呢？

Words of Wisdom

You don't face your fears. You stand up to them!

Look on the Bright Side

Always look on the bright side of things.

Someone left you? What's yours cannot be taken away. Now that he or she is gone, you can move on and find someone else who will make you happier.

Lost your job? It's normal to switch[1] jobs. This crisis[2] can be an opportunity to find a better one!

Sick? Fear only makes things worse. Face your illness. Deal with it, accept it, and live your life the best that you can.

Afraid that people will know the facts? Honesty is always the best policy. Courage is good, too. It's better that the truth comes out sooner rather than later.

Many things in life are beyond your control. However, one thing you can always control is how you react.

重要字彙

① switch [swɪtʃ] (v.) 轉移
② crisis [ˈkraɪsɪs] (n.) 危機

UNIT 45 都是自己嚇自己

戴爾卡內基曾經做過調查，發現我們為未來所擔憂的事情，百分之九十九都不會發生。但是很不幸，許多人卻天天生活在未來裡，自己嚇自己！

人生實在很短，浮生若夢，飛逝即過，我和姊姊、妹妹一起走路上小學的日子好像就在不久以前，怎麼一眨眼，都變成老婦了？活過了大半歲月的人應該同意，恐懼是人生的頭號殺手！因為在恐懼中，沒有喜樂。**沒了喜樂，窮人、富人、天才、蠢材都一樣可悲。**

除了自己，沒有什麼能真正嚇倒我們！

Words of Wisdom

Fear breeds fear.
　　　　　　　滋育

Never Live in Fear

According to Dale Carnegie's research, 99% of the things that people are afraid of will never happen. Unfortunately, many of us still live in self-fabricated[1] fear.

Time flies so fast, and life is like a dream. It seems like just yesterday when I was walking to elementary school[2] with my sisters, but now all of us have become old women! I believe those who have lived a long life agree that life is not worth living if it is lived in fear.

Let go of your fears and enjoy life!

重要字彙

① fabricate [ˈfæbrɪˌket] (v.) 編出來
② elementary school [ˌɛləˈmɛntərɪ skul] (n.) 小學

一、填充

How can we react?

1. Someone left you?

    ↓ What's yours cannot be taken away.

    所以：You can move on and

2. Lost your job?

    ↓ It's normal to switch jobs.

    所以：

3. Sick?

    ↓ Fear only makes things worse.

    所以：

4. Many things in life are beyond your control.

    ↓ Fortunately,

    one thing that you can always control is

二、Crossword Puzzles

請將以下所提示的英文單字填入字謎：

1. 心跳加快 (t...p)，必要的 (e...l)，情緒 (e...n)，談判 (n...e)，宣傳 *n.*
   (p...a)，毒性 (t...n)

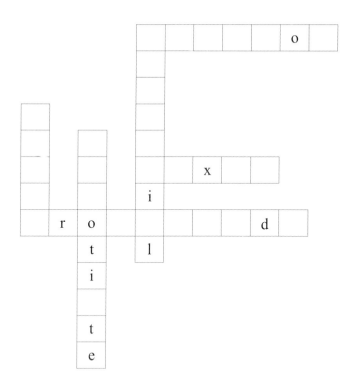

2. 編織 (f...e)，危機 (c...s)，轉換 (s...h)，有彈性的 (f...e)，甜點 (d...t)

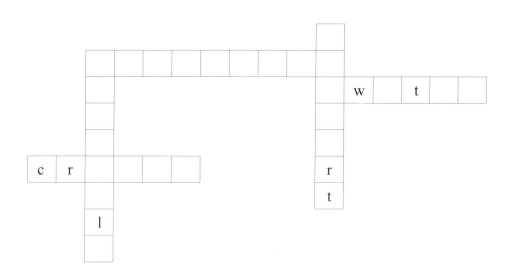

答案

一、填充

1. find someone else who will make you happier.

2. This crisis is an opportunity to find a better job!

3. Face your illness. Deal with it, accept it, and live your life the best that you can.

4. how you react.

二、Crossword Puzzles

1. **Across** emotion, toxin, propaganda

   Down thump, negotiate, essential

2. **Across** fabricate, switch, crisis

   Down flexible, dessert

Notes . . .

這才是真自由

有些行為看似自由，卻禁不起歲月的考驗：

我們有吹牛、作弊的自由，不過這種自由都有後遺症——沒有後遺症的才是真自由。

我們有做第三者的自由，也有劈腿的自由，但是這種自由會帶給別人痛苦——損人而利己的自由不是真自由，那是「自私」。

我們有今朝有酒今朝醉的自由，也有寅吃卯糧的自由，但是這種自由必然是短暫的——持久的才是真自由。

真自由使人心平氣和、問心無愧、眉開眼笑，並且真自由是長存的。

Words of Wisdom

Our ultimate freedom is the right and power to decide how anybody or anything outside ourselves will affect us.
➡ 意指：如果我們能自行決定是否受到別人的影響，就是自由！

Now, This Is True Freedom!

Some acts have consequences that are revealed only after the passage of time.

It is true that we have the freedom to brag[1] or cheat. Unfortunately, exercise of this kind of freedom can have negative[2] consequences.[3] Any freedom which may be followed with problems is not true freedom.

We have the freedom to be the third person in a relationship, just as we have the freedom to cheat on our loved ones. Any kind of freedom that brings pain and suffering to us or others is not true freedom.

We have the freedom to overindulge[4] in food and drink and spend tomorrow's money. Unfortunately, this kind of freedom is transient.[5] Any freedom that does not last is not true freedom.

What is true freedom? It is enjoying peace, happiness, and a clear conscience.[6]

重要字彙

① brag [bræg] (v.) 吹牛
② negative [ˈnɛgətɪv] (adj.) (v.) 否定的、負面的
③ consequence [ˈkɑnsəˌkwɛns] (n.) 結果
④ overindulge [ˌovɚɪnˋdʌldʒ] (v.) 沉溺
⑤ transient [ˈtrænʃənt] (adj.) 稍縱即逝的
⑥ conscience [ˈkɑnʃəns] (n.) 良心

被中傷是常態

　　被人中傷了，沒什麼大不了，我們絕對不是唯一被別人中傷的人。倒是要想一下，他說的有沒有道理？有過則改，無過則不用在意——嘴巴長在他臉上，他有絕對的權力決定要說什麼話。同時，耳朵長在我們自己的頭上，也只有自己有權力決定要不要聽！

　　一笑置之吧！何況，我們沒在背後說過人家嗎？一生之中，有一兩個人喜歡我們，就很不錯了。

Words of Wisdom

謗言　殺　　　　　　　　　　　說者　　　　聽者
Slander slays three people: the speaker, the spoken to, and the spoken of.
被說者

Just Laugh it Off!

• •

Gossip[1] is a normal part of life. Anywhere there is society, there is gossip and rumor.[2]

The first thing you should do when you hear a rumor about yourself is to reflect on[3] where it may have originated.[4] Is it true? Have I done something to deserve it? If so, make your amends.[5] If not, be content to know that you may not be able to control what other people say, but you can control what you hear and whom you talk to. If you cannot avoid the silly things people are saying about you, just dismiss[6] them with a laugh! After all, you are probably guilty[7] of talking behind someone's back at some point in your life, too!

We are lucky if we go through life and meet one or two people who truly like and understand us.

重要字彙

① gossip [ˈgɑsəp] (n.) (v.) 八卦
② rumor [ˈrumə] (n.) 謠言
③ reflect on (v.) 反省
④ originate [əˈrɪdʒəˌnet] (v.) 來自
⑤ make amends [əˈmɛnds] 修正
⑥ dismiss [dɪsˈmɪs] (v.) 解散
⑦ guilty [ˈgɪltɪ] (adj.) 有罪、內疚的

一、Crossword Puzzles

請將以下所提示的英文單字填入字謎：

1. 吹牛 (b...g)，結果 (c...e)，負面的 (n...e)，沉溺 (o...e)，良知 (c...e)，
   肝臟 (l...r)

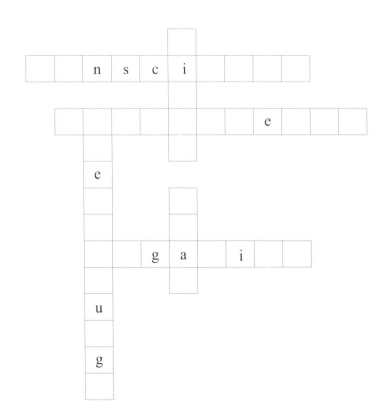

2. 八卦 (g...p)，謠言 (r...r)，小說 (f...n)，源自 (o...e)，修正 (a...d)，解散 (d...s)

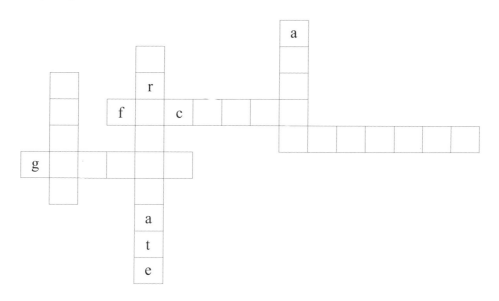

 答案

1. **Across** conscience, consequence, negative
   Down overindulge, liver, brag
2. **Across** fiction, dismiss, gossip
   Down rumor, originate, amend

UNIT 48 不輕易承諾

英文現在有一句一點都不好笑的幽默語：　"Promises are made to be broken."

雖然只是一句玩笑話，卻破壞了我們在社會立足最珍貴的根基：「真誠」，讓彼此失去互信。

這個社會仍然敬重言而有信之人；**言而無信的人，在工作和戀愛上，根本沒有機會**，這種人縱使一時被人信任，也終將失利。隨便承諾，就像給自己脖子上綁了一根韁繩，被用力地拖扯。

一旦承諾，就守著它，這是成功的基礎，也正是可敬的人性。

Words of Wisdom

A promise is a debt.

債

Always Keep Your Promises

• •

Contemporary English contains a humorous phrase that isn't funny at all: "Promises are made to be broken." The prevalence[1] of this saying shows how rare it is to find someone who can be trusted to keep a promise.

People who are sincere and honest are still highly esteemed.[2] Those who make promises lightly[3] will find themselves in big trouble in both work and romance[4] when it's discovered that they cannot be trusted.

A promise is to be kept once it's made. A person who is true to one's word will find that others will find him or her trustworthy,[5] reliable,[6] and worthy of praise.[7]

重要字彙

① prevalence [ˋprɛvələs] (n.) 漫延
② esteem [ɪsˋtim] (v.) 推崇
③ lightly [ˋlaɪtlɪ] (adv.) 輕易地
④ romance [roˋmæns] (n.) 戀愛
⑤ trustworthy [ˋtrʌstˏwɝðɪ] (adj.) 令人信任的
⑥ reliable [rɪˋlaɪəbḷ] (adj.) 可靠的
⑦ praise [prez] (n.) (v.) 稱讚

UNIT 49 尊重無形的資產

眼前的豪宅、名車、美貌、高學歷是有形的資產,價值很容易就被認定。曾經有過的資產則是無形的,價值通常被忽略。

退伍的將官、過氣的藝人、退休的學者、遲暮的美人、破產的富豪,他們所擁有的資產則是他們的「過去」。雖說這些已如過眼雲煙,不值得一提,但我們不妨有一點人情味,一起聊聊他們曾經擁有的燦爛。

Words of Wisdom

駿馬　　　　　　　馬舍　　　　渴望
An aged steed confined to the stable still aspires after the glory of galloping a thousand miles.
奔馳

Recognize[1] Intangible[2] Assets[3]

● ●

Things such as expensive houses, luxurious[4] cars, beauty, and prestigious[5] education are tangible[6] assets that are easily acknowledged. However, there are many intangible assets that are often overlooked.[7]

A retired general, an old movie star, a retired scholar, and a bankrupt businessman all have experiences and accomplishments that can be seen as intangible assets.

There is a lot to learn from the past, and these intangible assets may prove to be as valuable as any tangible asset you're likely to come across. Why don't we talk about their glory days?

重要字彙

① recognize [ˈrɛkəɡˌnaɪz] (v.) 認出
② intangible [ɪnˈtændʒəbl̩] (adj.) 無形的
③ asset [ˈæsɛt] (n.) 財產
④ luxurious [lʌɡˈʒʊrɪəs] (adj.) 奢侈的
⑤ prestigious [prɛsˈtɪdʒɪəs] (adj.) 知名的
⑥ tangible [ˈtændʒəbl̩] (adj.) 有形的
⑦ overlook [ˌovəˈlʊk] (v.) 忽略、眺望、前瞻

UNIT 50 人至察則無友

有些人眼光獨到，能見到人所不見，因此思緒通達、口才便給、分析精闢、並能迅速看到別人的弱點。這種人在群體中，往往是最有貢獻的人物。

不幸的是，這種人往往也是最寂寞的，因為大多數的人喜歡和柔軟、隨和、甚至有一絲糊塗的人相處，因為這樣的人不給人壓力！

水至清則無魚，人至察則無友。最聰明的人絕對不是最可愛的人！

Words of Wisdom

木屑
"Why do you look at the speck in your brother's eye but do not perceive the plank in your own eye?"
木板
~the Bible

Sometimes the Sharpest Minds Acquire[1] the Fewest Friends

· ·

Some people are so smart and perceptive[2] that they see what others cannot. They are quick, eloquent,[3] analytical,[4] and can find fault in any plan or situation. These people can contribute much to a project or business plan.

Unfortunately, they are also often lonely because most people like to be with people who are gentle and easy-going.

Just as extremely clean water cannot keep fish, extremely perceptive people cannot keep friends. Being a smart person is not the same as being a pleasant person.

重要字彙

① acquire [əˋkwaɪr] (v.) 取得
② perceptive [pəˋsɛptɪv] (adj.) 有觀察力的
③ eloquent [ˋɛləkwənt] (adj.) 口才便給的
④ analytical [͵ænḷˋɪtɪkḷ] (adj.) 會分析的

意志堅定的人，能說「不」

幫助人必能增加生命的亮度，但是助人最好乾乾脆脆、誠誠懇懇。**我們對於已答應的事情要全力去做、樂意去做；對於難以答應的事情，則不拖泥帶水地拒絕。**

向人說「不」當然不容易，但是與其心不甘情不願地勉強答應，之後又庸人自擾，弄得彼此傷了感情，還不如一開始就明白地拒絕。

往往，我們之所以難以說「不」，並不是因為我們特別有義氣，而是因為我們懦弱。

意志堅定一點，不懂得拒絕的人，經常忙了半天，還被笑是傻子。

Words of Wisdom

Better a friendly refusal than an unwilling promise.

拒絕

Say "NO!" Politely but Firmly

Helping people adds light to our lives, but we should be positive and sincere when we help. We should fulfill our promises with full devotion and pleasure, and reject with certainty things that we can do nothing about.

It's never easy to say "no", but if the truth is that we can't or don't want to do something, it is best to say so politely but firmly.

一、翻譯

1. 有一句俗話：「做承諾的目的是為了破壞它！」

   There is a _____, " _____ _____

   _____ _____ _____ _____."

2. 誠懇而誠實的人，仍受到大家高度地推崇。

   People who are _____ and _____ are still

   _____ _____.

3. 不要隨便做承諾。

   Do not _____ _____ I _____.

4. 一旦承諾，就信守到底。

   A _____ is t _____ b _____ k _____

   o _____ _____ m _____.

5. 他值得相信、做事可靠、令人欣賞。

   He is _____, _____, and w _____ of

   p _____.

6. 一旦承諾，就要全心全意、高高興興地做到！

   We s _____ f _____ o _____ p _____

   w _____ f _____ d _____ and p _____.

7. 如果我們實在做不到，就應該明確地拒絕！

   We s _____ r _____ w _____ c _____

   th _____ t _____ w _____ c _____

<u>d   n   a   </u>.

8. 我已經很禮貌而確定地拒絕他了。

I already _____ him _____ and _____.

二、Crossword Puzzles

請將以下所提示的英文單字填入字謎：

1. 認出 (r...e)，無形的 (i...e)，資產 (a...t)，奢華的 (l...s)，有名的 (p...s)，有形的 (t...e)，前瞻 (o...k)

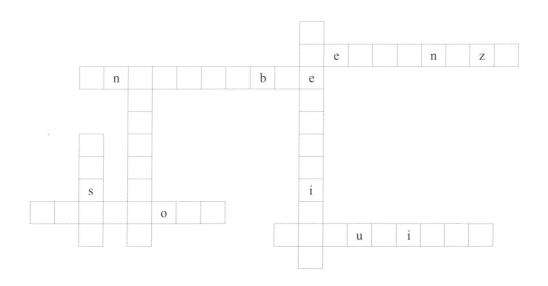

2. 要求 (a...e)，口才好的 (e...t)，有分析力的 (a...l)，觀察入微的 (p...e)，
   讚美 (p...e)，隨便地 (l...y)

答案

一、翻譯

1. saying, Promises are made to be broken

2. sincere, honest, highly esteemed

3. make promises lightly

4. promise, to be kept once it's made

5. trustworthy, reliable, worthy, praise

6. should fulfill our promises with full devotion, pleasure

7. should reject with certainty things that we can do nothing about

8. rejected, politely, firmly

二、Crossword Puzzles

1. **Across** recognize, intangible, overlook, luxurious

   Down asset, tangible, prestigious

2. **Across** praise, analytical, lightly

   Down acquire, eloquent, perceptive

珍惜批評

醫生診察我們的身體，給一些建議，使我們更健康——我們感激他，還付上診療費。

老師挑出我們學習上的失誤，並給予指導，使我們的程度更好——我們感謝老師，也付了學費。

其他方面的呢？言談、舉止、儀容、交友、工作，誰能指出我們的不足呢？大多數的人不願指出我們的不當之處。

我們要珍惜批評，將別人的批評視為極致珍寶，快樂地面對批評，才會一天比一天好。

Words of Wisdom

冷漠
The most destructive criticism is indifference.

Appreciate Criticisms[1]

. . . .

Doctors examine our health and give advice. We thank them and pay the treatment fee.

Teachers grade our assignments[2] and give advice. We thank them and pay tuition.[3]

What about in other parts of our lives? From behavior to appearance, work, and interpersonal[4] relationships, who can—and will—point out our shortcomings?

Appreciate criticism and use it to improve yourself. Constructive[5] criticism—the type that we can use to make ourselves better—is as precious as gold.

重要字彙

① criticism [ˋkrɪtəˏsɪzəm] (n.) 批評
② assignment [əˋsaɪnmənt] (n.) 工作
③ tuition [tjuˋɪʃən] (n.) 學費
④ interpersonal [ˏɪntəˋpɝsənl] (adj.) 人際的
⑤ constructive [kənˋstrʌktɪv] (adj.) 建設性的

免費的建設沒人甩

真言比真金珍貴。可惜,大多數的人只喜歡聽好話,不喜歡聽真話。

除非我們的工作的性質就是專業的批評,否則,不要自以為義,喜歡給人「良心的批評」。

通常,免費的東西再好,也不被珍惜。

Words of Wisdom

Unwanted advice is not appreciated.

Don't Give Unwanted Advice

Even though the truth is worth more than gold, most people only want to hear nice things. Unless you are a professional critic[1] or someone seeks your advice, it's best to keep your thoughts to yourself.

Don't be self-righteous.[2] People don't appreciate the things that they get for free, regardless of how good they are.

① critic [ˈkrɪtɪk] (n.) 批評家
② self-righteous [sɛlf ˈraɪtʃəs] (adj.) 自以為是的

UNIT 54 二比一法則

　　我們即使受人之託而善意地給予建議或批評，也須遵守「二比一法則」：先肯定兩次，再批評一次。例如：

　　如果他正在學英語，但是說話不夠清楚，我們可以這麼說：你的聲音很好聽、儀態也很好，如果口齒再清晰一點，就更棒了！

　　如果他的脾氣太大，我們可以這麼說：你很率真、也很熱心，如果脾氣再好一些，就更可愛！

　　如果他太吝嗇，我們可以這麼說：你很上進、也很活潑，如果再大方一些，就更容易成功！

　　為職業所需而給人批評建議的人，包括父母對孩子，別忘了二比一法則。

Words of Wisdom

Praise makes a good person better, and blame makes a bad one worse.

A Golden Rule: 2 to 1

I would suggest a 2:1 rule to those who are expected to comment or give advice (including parents): two positives for every negative.

For example, if someone is learning English but has unclear pronunciation, we can use this rule by saying, "You've got a beautiful voice and very nice posture,[1] but your performance would be even better if you could speak with more clarity.[2]"

Or if someone has a bad temper, we can use the 2:1 rule by saying, "You're outspoken[3] and passionate.[4] You can be very charming when you control your temper."

Or if someone is stingy, we can say, "You're hard-working and lively, but a little more generosity would be even better."

For every negative thing that you have to say, balance it out with two positive things.

重要字彙

---

① posture [ˈpɑstʃɚ] (n.) 儀態
② clarity [ˈklærətɪ] (n.) 清晰度
③ outspoken [autˈspokən] (adj.) 率直的
④ passionate [ˈpæʃənɪt] (adj.) 熱情的

一、Crossword Puzzles

請將以下所提示的英文單字填入字謎：

1. 作業 (a...t)，學費 (t...n)，人際間的 (i...l)，批評 *n.* (c...m)，有建設性的 (c...e)

											c
		c				c	i				
n		r	e					g			
		t									
		u		t		n					

2. 儀態 (p...e)，清晰 *n.* (c...y)，率直的 (o...n)，熱情的 (p...e)，批評者
(c...c)

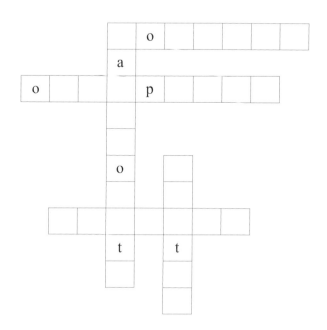

 答案

1. **Across** criticism, interpersonal, tuition
   Down constructive, assignment
2. **Across** posture, outspoken, clarity
   Down passionate, critic

UNIT 55　媒體是強勢的推銷員

在馬路上，如果有人向我們推銷商品，我們不見得會買，因為我們可能會排斥這種推銷。但是我們卻被「無形」的推銷給打垮了——這個最強勢的推銷員，就是「媒體」。

下次看到媒體上的商品時，想一想：我是不是又再被它洗腦了？

Words of Wisdom

Strong souls have willpower, and weak ones only desire.

意志

Are You a "Yes-Man" to Mass Media?

We may easily reject salespeople who approach[1] us on the street, but we often surrender[2] without knowing it to the ultimate[3] salesman: mass media.

The next time you think about making a purchase[4] based on a radio, newspaper, magazine, Internet, or TV advertisement, think to yourself, "Am I being brainwashed again?"

重要字彙

① approach [ə`protʃ] (v.) 接近
② surrender [sə`rɛndə] (v.) 投降
③ ultimate [`ʌltəmɪt] (adj.) 最後的、終極的
④ purchase [`pɜtʃəs] (n.) 購買

UNIT 56 你是名牌的主人，還是奴隸？

我一直感覺，有兩種人似乎是名牌的死忠擁護者：

一種人對物品偏執，另一種人則缺乏自信。

許多對物品偏執的人非拿名牌不可，因為這種人比較軟弱，無法戰勝商品的誘惑。

許多缺乏自信的人很喜歡用名牌，因為需要外在的物品來增加自己的價值。

很遺憾，這兩種人，都乖乖地被名牌使喚。

無論富裕與否，不看重名牌的人，才是掌控名牌魅力的人。

Words of Wisdom

Hunger goes in a straight line, and desire turns in circles.

欲望

Who's the Boss?

Two kinds of people seem to be obsessed[1] with brand names: one is obsessed with material things, and the other lacks confidence.

— Those who are obsessed with material things tend to be vain[2] and weak.

— Those who lack confidence are likely to buy brand-name products because they need something to affirm[3] their own value. Both types of people are slaves to objects.

Those who can see beyond the logos[4] on brand-name products are truly smart.

重要字彙

① obsessed [əb`sɛst] (*adj.*) 執著的
② vain [ven] (*adj.*) 愛虛榮的
③ affirm [ə`fɝm] (*v.*) 確認、肯定
④ logo [`logo] (*n.*) 商標

面子是害人精

　　有些人長期受「面子」所奴役，日子過得真辛苦。既然「面子」是給別人看的，我們如果為了別人而打腫自己的臉充胖子，不就是為別人而活？

　　一個口袋多金的人，身邊朋友必定不少，但是這並不神氣，因為錢買來的朋友會隨時消失，毫無價值。一個位居要職的人，身邊親信也不會少，但是這也不派頭，因為會繞在權勢之旁的人，不是真朋友。

　　錢和權所買來的面子，只顯出我們真正的貧乏。真的東西才可貴，而真正的情誼超越富貧與美醜。如果我們不再理會面子，而認真扮演好自己的角色，自然就會很有面子！

Words of Wisdom

Much money, many friends.

Are You Obsessed with "Face"?

Face is closely related to pride and vanity.[1] Many people spend their whole lives keeping face.

But this type of face is merely for the benefit[2] of other people. Anyone whose goal is to maintain face has lost his or her freedom in the world.

People with lots of money often have many people hanging around them, but these fair-weather friends are nothing to be proud of because once the good times are gone, so are they. The same is true for someone in a high position of power. Their supporters are drawn to the power; and they are not true friends.

Face that is gained with money or position is fleeting.[3] If you stop worrying about face and put all your effort into being a responsible person, your face will naturally take care of itself.

重要字彙

① vanity [ˈvænətɪ] (n.) 虛榮
② benefit [ˈbɛnəfɪt] (n.) 利益
③ fleet [ˈflit] (v.) 流逝

不要瞎模仿

有錢人開名車是「享受」，窮人開名車則是「自找罪受」。

有錢人穿名牌是「品味」，窮人穿名牌則是「安慰」。

有錢人去高級餐廳是「吃飯」，窮人去高級餐廳則是「吃面子」。

雖然有錢人有許多朋友，但較難得到真愛和真友誼；窮人朋友少，但所得到的卻多是真愛和真朋友——我們何必裝闊呢？

Words of Wisdom

Don't imitate the butterfly before you have wings.

Be Yourself

• •

Rich people can afford luxury cars,[1] brand-name clothing, and expensive food.

In today's materialistic[2] culture, it's cool to have all these expensive things. However, you shouldn't try to imitate[3] a lifestyle that you can't afford. Rich or poor, we are entitled to[4] true love and true friendships. There's absolutely no need to pretend to be rich.

重要字彙

① luxury car 名車（也可說 luxurious car）
② materialistic [mə͵tɪrɪəl`ɪstɪk] (*adj.*) 物質的
③ imitate [`ɪmə͵tet] (*v.*) 模仿
④ be entitled to + (n.) 有資格……

一、翻譯

1. 有錢人可以買名車、穿名牌、吃高檔美食。

R_____ p_____ c_____ a_____

l_____ c_____, b_____-n_____

c_____, and e_____ f_____.

2. 我們不該模仿別人，過一個超出我們能力的生活。

We shouldn't try to i_____ a l_____ that we

c_____ a_____.

3. 真愛與真友誼不受物質左右。

T_____ l_____ and t_____ f_____

do not c_____ f_____ m_____ t_____.

二、Crossword Puzzles

請將以下所提示的英文單字填入字謎：

1. 接近 (a...h)，投降 (s...r)，最終的 (u...e)，購買 (p...e)，流逝的 (f...g)

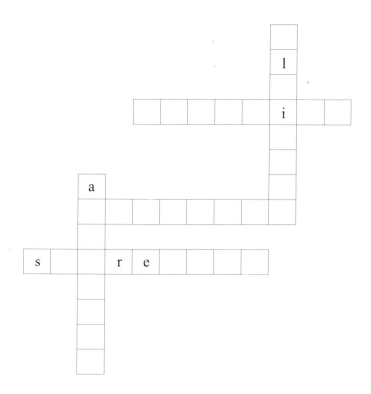

2. 執著的 (o...d)，虛榮的 (v...n)，膚淺 (s...w)，肯定 (a...m)，標誌 (l...o)，貢獻 (c...e)

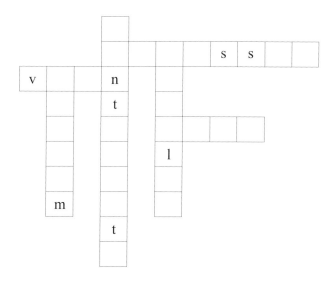

答案

一、翻譯

1. Rich people can afford luxury cars, brand-name clothing, expensive food

2. imitate, lifestyle, can't afford

3. True love, true friendships, come from material things

二、**Crossword Puzzles**

1. **Across** fleeting, purchase, surrender

   Down approach, ultimate

2. **Across** obsessed, vain, logo

   Down affirm, contribute, shallow

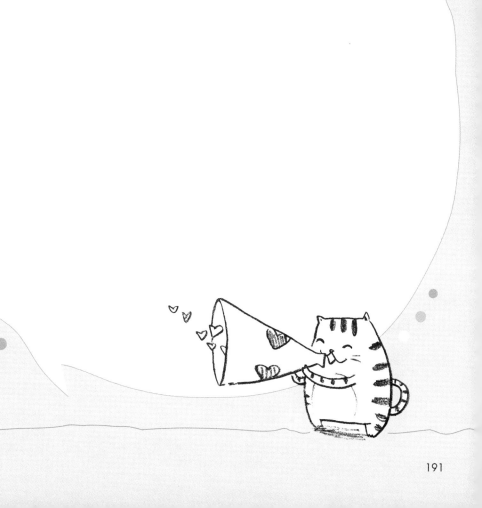

三人行必有我師

我們都很渺小，沒什麼好自傲的：一個不小心就會感冒、摔一跤就可能折斷骨頭、再聰明的人也會做傻事、再美麗的臉龐也會老去、再富裕的人也有所不足。

所以，無論我們看起來有多棒，別人必有勝過我們之處！

每一個人都具獨特性。只要我們謙卑柔和，必可看到別人的長處；不斷地學習別人的長處，我們當然就不斷地進步！

Words of Wisdom

The more noble the more humble.
　　尊貴　　　　　　謙卑

There Is Always Something to Learn from Another Person

We are actually quite vulnerable. A chill may bring us a cold, and a fall may break our bones. Even the smartest people make mistakes, and the most beautiful faces will age.[1] Even people with enormous bank accounts can feel poor in other ways. Thus, we should always remain humble.

Humble people respect the merits[2] of others. Everyone has his or her own unique individuality. We can always learn from others if we are humble enough. Of course, a great way to improve yourself is to constantly adopt the merits of other people.

重要字彙

① age [edʒ] (v.) 老化
② merit [ˋmɛrɪt] (n.) 優點

找對人

要買五金，該去五金行，而非水果店。

要快樂，該向樂觀的人請教。

要賺錢，該向富人請教。

要認真地交異性朋友，該向感情幸福穩定的人請教。

要闖天下，該向勇敢積極的人請教，因為保守退縮的人只會潑冷水。

找對人，才能做對事，而且做得快又好。

Words of Wisdom

What's the use of running when we are on the wrong road?

Go to the Right Person

If we need to buy hardware,¹ we go to a hardware store, not a fruit shop.

If we wish to find happiness, we should consult a very happy person.

If we wish to become rich, we need to consult a rich person.

If we wish to have a successful romance, we should consult someone who has a happy and successful relationship.

If we wish to blaze our own trail,² we should consult someone who is brave and ambitious because a conservative person will only discourage us.

No matter what it is that you need or want to know, start off by talking to the right person. Otherwise, you could end up being pointed in the wrong direction.

重要字彙

① hardware [ˋhɑrdˌwɛr] (n.) 五金
② blaze one's own trail 闖天下

益友

　　孔子說過：「友直、友諒、友多聞。」因為這樣的朋友可以幫助我們成為更好的人。然而，並非人人皆可得到這樣的朋友，而且，如果所有的朋友皆如此，生活也太嚴肅了。

　　我們不妨重新詮釋「友多聞」。如果一個人讓我們認識生命的藝術、如果一個人澆灌我們喜樂的心、如果一個人讓我們生活地更健康，他們的知識早就超越了書本，他們是真正的「友多聞」。

Words of Wisdom

Better one true friend than a hundred relatives.

Appreciate Beneficial Friends

Although Confucius once said, "Make friends with those who are outspoken, forgiving and knowledgeable," not everyone is able to meet people with these qualities. Besides, would you really enjoy it if all your friends were like this?

We may reinterpret "friends who are knowledgeable." When someone leads us to see something that we never realized before, brings cheerfulness into our lives, or makes us healthier, he or she has improved our lives using knowledge that can't be found in books. This type of knowledgeable friend is truly the most valuable.

UNIT 62 從三件事認清一個人

三個行為準則可以幫助我們輕鬆而準確地認清一個人。

1. 他得意之時，胸懷如何？——如果他謙柔待人、樂於助人，就是「大度」之人。

2. 他工作失意時，情操如何？——如果他努力扭轉劣勢、並且不貪非分之財，就是「有骨氣、有操守」之人。

3. 他對錢的態度如何？——在許多珍貴的東西中，唯一可以去了又被拿回的，大概就只有金錢了。因此，一個人如果連小錢都吝於付出，就沒什麼不會計較的了。

Words of Wisdom

Anyone can be polite to a king, but it takes a good person to be polite to a beggar.

From Three Things We Can Know a Person

• •

Three behavioristic[1] norms[2] may help us easily identify[3] with a person.

1. How does the person treat people when he or she is successful? If humble, friendly, and willing to help, this is a decent[4] person.
2. How does the person act when he or she is in dire straits?[5] If the person works hard to turn the tide[6] and does not take what doesn't belong to him or her, this is a person of decency.
3. How does the person treat money? While many things in life are irreplaceable, money is not one of them. If a person is stingy with money, then he or she will be stingy with everything.

重要字彙

① behavioristic [bɪˌhevjəˋrɪstɪk] (*adj.*) 行為上的
② norm [nɔrm] (*n.*) 基準
③ identify [aɪˋdɛntəˌfaɪ] (*v.*) 確認
④ decent [ˋdisn̩t] (*adj.*) 正派的
⑤ in dire straits (*prep. phrase*) 落魄的
⑥ turn the tide (*v.*) 扭轉劣勢

一、填充

A. We should always remain humble because we are all quite vulnerable:

1. A chill

   ↓ may

2. A fall

   ↓ may

3. Even the smartest people

   ↓ may

4. The most beautiful face

   ↓ will

5. Even people with enormous bank accounts

   ↓ can

B. No matter what we need to know, start off going to the right place：

1. If we need to buy hardware,

   ↓

2. If we wish to find happiness,

   ↓

3. If we wish to become rich,

   ↓

4. If we wish to have a successful romance,

   ↓

二、翻譯

1. 孔子曾說：「友直、友諒、友多聞。」

   C_____ o_____ said, "M_____ f_____

   w_____ t_____ w_____ _____

   _____, _____ and _____."

2. 我們可以重新詮釋「成功」。

   We may _____ "_____."

3. 這些提供了讓我們活得更好，卻在書中找不到的知識。

These i_____ o___ _____ l_____ u___

a k_____ that c_____ b_____ f___

i_____ b_____.

三、Crossword Puzzle

請將以下所提示的英文單字填入字謎：行為上的 (b...c)，規範 (n...m)，

指認 (i...y)，有格調的 (d...t)

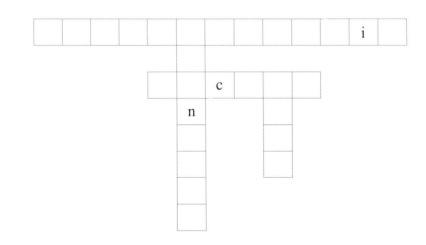

答案

一、填充

A.

1. bring us a cold.

2. break our bones.

3. make mistakes.

4. age.

5. feel poor in other ways.

B.

1. go to a hardware store

2. consult a very happy person

3. consult a rich man

4. consult someone who has a happy relationship

二、翻譯

1. Confucius once, Make friends with those who are outspoken, forgiving, knowledgeable

2. reinterpret success

3. improve our lives using, knowledge, can't be found in books

三、Crossword Puzzle

Across behavioristic, decent

Down identify, norm

愛的教育、鐵的紀律

　　成功的父母給予孩子百分之百的愛和百分之百的紀律。紀律就是一個看不到，卻堅硬無比的框，在這個框內，孩子自由自在、無拘無束，玩瘋了也無妨，但絕不可超越這個範圍。

　　父母就是這個框，給孩子完全的保護，讓他們不至於走了樣。這樣的孩子最幸福，也最有安全感，以後可順利適應社會。

Words of Wisdom

If you think education is expensive, try ignorance!

Children Need Abundant Love and Strict Discipline

. . . .

A good parent should always educate his or her child with love and care. However, that doesn't mean a parent shouldn't be firm with discipline.[1] In fact, if you love your child, you should discipline him or her.

Society is filled with rules both written and unwritten.[2] Children thus need to be clear about rules. Parents provide structure within which a child can feel free and safe. At the same time, children need to know that they must not cross the line between right and wrong.

重要字彙

① discipline [ˈdɪsəplɪn] (*n.*)(*v.*) 紀律
② unwritten [ʌnˈrɪtn̩] (*adj.*) 沒寫下的

UNIT 64　孩子的福祉在父母手中

小孩子被燙著了——因為父母粗心。

孩子交友不慎——因為父母沒有早日培養孩子自行判斷的能力。

「為人父母」是一生當中最長、最辛苦的一個工作。但是**認真的父母必有甜美的回報**。

Words of Wisdom

Children yoke parents to the past, present, and future.

使羈絆

You Are Responsible for Your Child's Wellbeing

Good parents must take responsibility for their children.

If parents are not vigilant,[1] their children could get hurt.

If parents don't provide guidance, their children will make poor choices.

The best thing a parent can do is to give a child the ability to make good decisions and know right from wrong.

A parent's job is long and hard, but fortunately successful parents are definitely rewarded.[2]

重要字彙

① vigilant [`vɪdʒələnt] (adj.) 警惕的
② reward [rɪ`wɔrd] (v.)(n.) 回饋

挖掘他們的長處

　　有些孩子實在讓人恨地牙癢癢的。其實，再可惡的孩子，都有他的可愛之處；再沒出息的孩子，也都有他的可造之處。

　　我小學的時候常幫助一個不愛讀書的男生做功課，但他考試一直是全班最後一名。三十年後，我去參加小學同學會，發現幾十位同學中，事業最成功的就是他。

　　不要放棄孩子。不愛讀書的小孩可能喜歡木工、跳舞、機器、運動──我們要找出他們的長處，栽培他們。

　　喜歡頂嘴的小孩雖然可惡，但是他們通常都蠻勇敢、頭腦靈巧、口才便給──他們以後可以成為一流的銷售員、教師、律師，甚至立法委員。

Find Their Merits

• •

The worst people can have some good qualities, and even the most unpromising[1] children may have some hidden talent.

When I was in elementary school, I often did homework for a boy who was not interested in studying and always got the worst grades in our class. I saw him at a class reunion[2] thirty years later, and he ended up being the most successful of us all.

Do not give up on your children. If they're not academically[3] inclined,[4] they may be gifted[5] in other areas such as carpentry,[6] dance, sports, or art. Just find out what they're good at and nurture their talent.

Children who like to talk back are irritating,[7] but they are also often brave, quick-minded and eloquent.[8] Such skills translate well to careers in sales, teaching, law, or even politics.

重要字彙

① unpromising [ʌn`prɑmɪsɪŋ] (adj.) 沒出息的

② reunion [ri`junjən] (n.) 團圓、再聯合

③ academically [ˌækə`dɛmɪkəlɪ] (adv.) 學術上、功課上

④ inclined [ɪn`klaɪnd] (adj.) 偏向的、依附的

⑤ gifted [gɪftɪd] (adj.) 有天資的

⑥ carpentry [`kɑrpəntrɪ] (n.) 木工藝

⑦ irritate [`ɪrəˌtet] (v.) 使腦怒

⑧ eloquent [`ɛləkwənt] (adj.) 雄辯的

親子之間不要太僵化，每個孩子都有他自己的一條路，但需要父母的鼓勵。何況出問題的通常是父母，而非孩子。**與其專心挑剔，不如努力地欣賞孩子。**

Parents and children teach one another.

Parents should be flexible. They should recognize[9] their children's strengths and encourage them to pursue[10] a life that they are suited for. When it comes to family conflict, the problem too often lies with the parents and not the child. Instead of concentrating on picking up after their children, parents should focus on praising them.

重要字彙

[9] recognize [ˈrɛkəgˌnaɪz] (v.) 認清
[10] pursue [pəˋsu] (v.) 尋求

他們是獨立的個體

　　我們之所以與孩子發生衝突，最大的原因是，我們認為他們應該走在我們的期望當中，而沒有把孩子視為獨立的個體。孩子不是父母的財產，我們只能養育他、協助他、教導他，其他的就隨他自己發展吧，**因為他們不是我們。**

　　如果孩子不喜歡讀書，我們就找出他們的興趣。條條大路通羅馬，讀書並非唯一的路。想想看，王永慶、郭台銘、比爾蓋茲有多少員工的學歷超過他們！

　　只要我們已對兒女盡了督導之責，就開始欣賞他們和我們之不同吧！

　　父母必須尊重子女各自的選擇，**因為他們是個別的生命體。**博士也好，工人也好，只要品行好，都好。

Words of Wisdom

Fruits of the same tree have different tastes; children of the same mother have various qualities.

Let Your Children Be Themselves

· ·

The major reason why parents have conflict[1] with children is that parents often look at their children as their property and thus expect their children to take the path that has been paved for them.

But children are definitely not the property of their parents. The job of parents is to raise, educate, and assist children and allow them to develop into their own unique person.

If your children are not so interested in studying, perhaps there is something else that inspires them. There are many roads to success. Just think, Bill Gates and Warren Buffett have many employees with higher degrees than they have.

As long as you maintain a basic level of guidance, feel free to just sit back and watch because it's time to appreciate!

Eventually parents must respect their children's choices because they are individual entities[2]—not property.

重要字彙

① conflict [ˈkɑnflɪkt] (n.)(v.) 衝突
② entity [ˈɛntətɪ] (n.) 實體

一、接句子

A. Good parents must take responsibility for their children.

1. Children get burned

   ↓ because

2. Children make poor choices in friends

   ↓ because

二、翻譯

A.

1. 即使最沒出息的孩子也有某些未被發現的長處。

   Even the most u_____ children may have some h_____

   t_____.

2. 他常考全班最低分。

   He often g_____ the w_____ g_____ in

   _____.

3. 我不喜歡讀書。

   I'm not a_____ i_____.

4. 我在某些方面有天份。

   I'm g_____ _____ some a_____.

5. 親子不合時，通常問題在於父母。

When it c_____ t_____ family c_____, too often

the problem l_____ w_____ the parents.

B.

1. 父母常認為孩子應該走在父母為他們安排的人生路途當中。

Parents often e_____ t_____ c_____ to

t_____ t_____ p_____ that h_____

b_____ p_____ f_____ t_____.

2. 父母的工作是幫助孩子自我發展。

The j_____ of the p_____ is to h_____

c_____ d_____ i_____ t_____

o_____ u_____ p_____.

3. 許多替比爾蓋茲和巴菲特工作的人，學歷比他們還高。

B_____ G_____ and W_____ B_____

have many e_____ w_____ h_____

d_____ than they have.

三、Crossword Puzzles

請將以下所提示的英文單字填入字謎：

1. 紀律 (d...e)，木工藝 (c...y)，口才好的 (e...t)，沒寫下來的 (u...n)

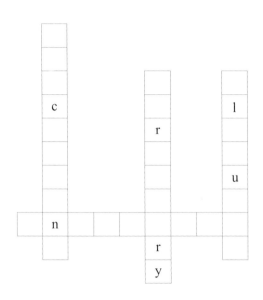

2. 警惕的 (v...t)，沒出息的 (u...g)，認清 (r...e)，有回報的 (r...d)，

衝突(c...t)

答案

一、接句子

1. the parent are not vigilant.

2. the parents do not provide guidance. (or do not give their children the ability to know right from wrong.)

二、翻譯

A.

1. unpromising, hidden talents

2. gets, worst grades, class

3. academically, inclined

4. gifted in, areas

5. comes to, conflict, lies with

B.

1. expect, their children, take the path, has been paved for them

2. job, parents, help children develop into their own unique person

3. Bill Gates, Warren Buffet, employees with higher degrees

三、Crossword Puzzles

1. **Across** unwritten

   Down discipline, carpentry, eloquent

2. **Across** unpromising, recognize

   Down conflict, rewarded, vigilant

人人平等　泰然自若

每一個人無論資質如何，境遇如何，都必有自己的長處。

一個清潔工和教授們在一起，理當泰然自若──因為他是他，我是我，各有貢獻。

一個瘦小的男生和一群高大的運動員在一起，理當泰然自若──因為他是他，我是我，各有所長。

一個小職員和一群成功的企業家在一起，理當泰然自若──因為他是他，我是我，各有職責。

他過他的日子，我過我的日子。他不欠我，我也不欠他，我們當然泰然自若！和人相處，不在於身分或財富，而在於一顆開闊坦蕩的心。

Words of Wisdom

He that is at ease seeks dainties.

平心靜氣　　　　典雅

We Are All Equal

* *

Everyone has some talent regardless of his or her background. No one is better than anyone else because of one's profession,[1] education, or wealth.

A janitor[2] can chat with a professor as an equal because all people are equal.

Someone who is short and thin can be comfortable around tall, muscle-bound bodybuilders,[3] because they are equal.

We are all born equal. No human being is worth more than another. Therefore, we should all be able to feel at ease no matter whom we are with. Disregard[4] status and let an open mind bring over friendships!

重要字彙

① profession [prəˋfɛʃən] (n.) 職業
② janitor [ˋdʒænɪtə] (n.) 清潔工
③ bodybuilder [ˋbɑdɪˌbɪldə] (n.) 健身教練
④ disregard [ˌdɪsrɪˋgɑrd] (v.) 不理會

UNIT 68 聲音是一張名片

要能夠沉得住氣，因為我們說話的口氣不但顯示我們的 EQ，甚至可以回過頭來，影響我們的心境。

被人冤枉時，不急不徐地說：「你冤枉我了，你最好先把事情弄清楚。」他是否道歉並不重要，重要的是，你已清楚地表達立場。

和人爭論時，口氣平靜若水地說：「我可以和你溝通，但不打算和你吵架。」──他是否溝通並不重要，重要的是，你的情緒已勝過他。

勇敢、沉著、冷靜、清楚地表達立場，你就掌握了全局。

Words of Wisdom

Lower your voice and strengthen your argument.

Tone Is Important

• •

The proper attitude, which would be conveyed[1] by an appropriate tone,[2] not only reveals[3] your EQ, but it can also affect your mood.

If you've been wronged[4] by someone, calmly let him or her know. He or she may not apologize, but you can rest easy knowing that you have done your part.

If you must argue in an unpleasant situation, just calmly say, "I would be happy to communicate with you, but I do not intend to fight with you." Your attitude will let this person know that you have taken the high road.

If you have stated[5] your position clearly, firmly and calmly, you have gained the upper hand.[6]

重要字彙

① convey [kənˋve] (v.) 傳達
② tone [ton] (n.) 口氣
③ reveal [rɪˋvil] (v.) 顯露
④ wrong [rɔŋ] (v.) 錯怪
⑤ state [stet] (v.) 陳述
⑥ gain the upper hand 占上風

替別人的成功鼓掌

　　如果我們都可以惜才愛才，讓每個人才都有機會貢獻所長，我們豈不是共創一個進步的社會？

　　看到漂亮的女孩，內心不要竊竊希望她失戀，讚美她吧！
　　看到富裕的人，內心不要竊竊希望他挫敗，替他高興吧！
　　看到聰明的人，內心不要竊竊希望他出糗，欣賞他吧！
　　看到幸福的人，內心不要竊竊希望他受苦，祝福他更好吧！

　　很少人會去詛咒一個窮又笨的人，但也很少人能真心地祝福一個比自己強的人，這就是人性的軟弱，我們要戰勝它。

　　為別人的成功而用力地鼓掌吧！

Words of Wisdom

Compete. Don't envy.

Applaud[1] the Talents and Success of Others

. . . .

We should respect and cherish the talents of others. The more people contribute[2] their talents to society, the better the world becomes.

We should not be jealous of beautiful women or handsome men. Their beauty should be appreciated.

We may wish poverty on the rich, but we should be happy for their financial[3] security.

We may wish failure on the intelligent[4] and the accomplished,[5] but we should appreciate the contributions that they make to the world.

Very few people would curse[6] someone who is poor and uneducated, but not many can applaud those who are superior.

Someone who can sincerely be happy for others will in turn be happier. Applaud loudly for the success of others!

重要字彙

① applaud [ə`plɔd] (v.) 向……鼓掌
② contribute [kən`trɪbjut] (v.) 貢獻
③ financial [faɪ`nænʃəl] (adj.) 金錢的

④ intelligent [ɪn`tɛlədʒənt] (adj.) 聰明的
⑤ accomplish [ə`kɑmplɪʃ] (v.) 成就
⑥ curse [kɜs] (v.) 詛咒

一、填充

1. 說話的口氣顯示我們的EQ。

   T_____ r_____ our EQ.

2. 你錯怪他了。

   You've _____ him.

3. 你該做的都做了。

   You have d_____ y_____ p_____.

4. 你比他強，因為你不和他計較。

   You have t_____ the h_____ r_____.

5. 我會清楚地陳述我的立場。

   I'll s_____ my p_____ clearly.

二、Crossword Puzzles

請將以下所提示的英文單字填入字謎：

1. 職業 (p...n)，清潔工 (j...r)，健身教練 (b...r)，不理會 (d...d)

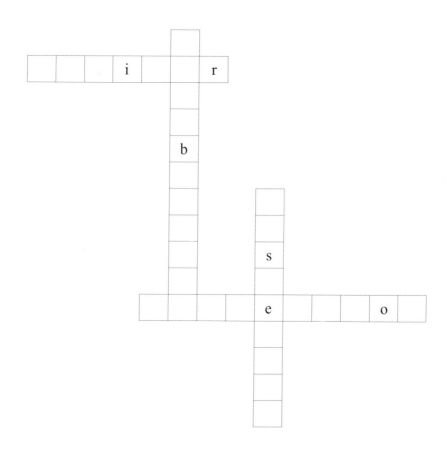

2. 鼓掌 *v.* (a...d)，貢獻 *v.* (c...e)，金錢的 (f...l)，揭露 (r...l)，聰明的 (i...t)

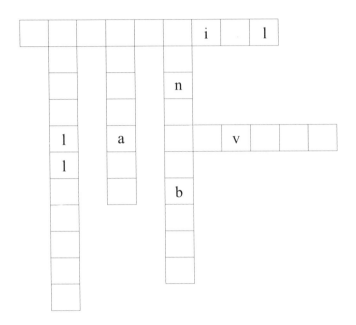

 答案

一、填充

1. Tone reveals

2. wronged

3. done your part

4. taken, high road

5. state, position

二、Crossword Puzzles

1. **Across** janitor, profession

   Down bodybuilder, disregard

2. **Across** financial, reveal

   Down intelligent, applaud, contribute

Notes...

227

UNIT 70 生涯規劃很重要

　　我們旅行有兩種方式，一種是預先規劃、穩當放心，另一種是隨興而去、盡興而返。

　　兩者各有利弊。前者可能少了刺激，卻多了安穩；後者多了刺激，卻少了安穩。

　　雖說人生如客旅，但是旅行和生命有所不同；我們可以多次旅行，這次不滿意，下次可以再來。生命卻不然，**因為我們只能活一次，所以這一次就要活得好！**

　　我們如果在年輕的時候，對人生就有所規劃，雖然生命常有意外的際遇，但是**我們之前的規劃，會像燈塔一樣，領著我們往前走，不致茫然。**

Words of Wisdom

He who fails to plan plans to fail.

Plan for the Future

· ·

There are two types of travel. The first is a prearranged[1] trip that is planned weeks or months in advance. It's safe and predictable.[2] The second is a spur-of-the-moment[3] trip. This type of travel is spontaneous[4] and exciting, but it is also riskier.

Although it's often said that the journey[5] of life is like traveling, there is one important difference: we can travel as many times as we like, but we can live only once.

Therefore, it is best to plan for your future when you are young. This way you can make sure that you don't get lost or end up not regretting during the later years of your life.

重要字彙

① prearrange [priə`rendʒ] (v.) 預先安排
② predictable [prɪ`dɪktəbl̩] (adj.) 可預料的
③ spur-of-the-moment (adj.) 一時衝動的
④ spontaneous [spɑn`tenɪəs] (adj.) 隨性的、自然流露的
⑤ journey [`dʒɜnɪ] (n.) 旅行

UNIT 71　規劃人生的前半段

　　浮生若夢，所幸，一般的夢是身不由己，而人生之夢，則可由我們自己編織：

- 童年——這是歡喜快樂、無憂、無慮的階段，應該多多玩樂。
- 青少年——這是學習力最強的階段，應該認真讀書或者學習一技之長。
- 畢業至三十歲左右——這尚不是真正賺錢的階段，所以重心放在學習社會經驗以及累積人脈，而且必需學會「觀察」、「判斷」與「表達」。
- 三十歲至中年——為家庭而工作，開始累積財富和人生智慧。

　　只要做好了規劃，如果沒有意外，我們的前半段人生應該不至於太差。

Words of Wisdom

A good plan today is better than a perfect plan tomorrow.

Plan for the First Half of Life

• •

Life is like a dream. The difference between real life and a dream is that we can't control our dreams in the way we can control our lives.

During childhood, a child's life should be happy and carefree:[1] full of joy and play.

During the teenage years is when the ability to learn is strongest, so teens should concentrate on[2] studying or honing[3] a specialty[4] or talent.

After graduating from high school or college to approximately[5] 30 years of age, instead of spending these precious young-adult years focusing on making money, young adults need to accumulate[6] social experiences and build interpersonal relationships[7] so that they can learn how to observe, make decisions, and express themselves clearly.

From age thirty to middle age, family should be the main focus. Work to provide wisdom and financial stability for your loved ones.

重要字彙

① carefree [ˈkɛrˌfri] (*adj.*) 無憂無慮
② concentrate on 專注於
③ hone [hon] (*v.*) 努力培養
④ specialty [ˈspɛʃəltɪ] (*n.*) 專業

⑤ approximately [əˈprɑksəmɪtlɪ] (*adv.*) 大約
⑥ accumulate [əˈkjumjəˌlet] (*v.*) 累積
⑦ interpersonal relationship(s) 人脈

規劃人生的後半段

我們前半段的人生接受社會的栽培,因此難免被社會的脈動所牽引;至於後半段,則可完全獨立於自己的手中:

一邊養生——運動、飲食、調息養氣。享受生命,並為老年做準備。

一邊回饋——把生活的重心從自己和兒女移轉到社會;把時間、金錢、智慧與人分享。

這兩項很重要,因為**如果注重養生,就不易生病,才能享受老年**。如果願意回饋,就不會有枯乾孤寂的老年,所擁有的將是一個充滿熱度、力度及亮度的老年!

Words of Wisdom

If you wish to sit in the shade during your old age, plant a tree now.

Plan for the Second Half of Life

The first half of life is largely directed by society. School and many other childhood experiences are mandatory,[1] and this isn't necessarily a bad thing. Moreover, the second half of life provides much more freedom for you to choose what you want to do.

— Take care of your health. Exercise, eat a proper diet, don't stress[2] yourself out, and prepare for old age.

— Give back to society. Switch the focus of life from you and the people around you to the needy.[3] Share your wealth and wisdom with others who are less fortunate.

If you have lived a good, generous life, you won't have to worry about being alone. You will be blessed with wonderful relationships and be surrounded by positivity.[4] This will enable[5] you to enjoy your golden years knowing that you have lived life to the fullest.

重要字彙

① mandatory [ˈmændəˌtorɪ] (adj.) 命令的、必要的
② stress [strɛs] (n.)(v.) 壓力
③ needy [ˈnidɪ] (adj.) 貧窮的
④ positivity [pɑzəˈtɪvətɪ] (n.) 正面、肯定
⑤ enable [ɪnˈebl̩] (vt.) 使能夠

一、填充

1. 我們應該在年少時即培養一技之長。

   We should h_____ some sort of s_____ as a teenager.

2. 我正在累積社會經驗。

   I'm a_____ social e_____.

3. 我們如何才能促進人際關係？

   How can we improve our i_____ r_____?

4. 你目前的重心應該在家庭。

   F_____ should be your m_____ f_____ now.

5. 孩童的日子應該無憂無慮。

   A c_____ life should be c_____.

二、Crossword Puzzles

請將以下所提示的英文單字填入字謎：

1. 旅程 (j...y)，預定安排 (p...e)，可被預測的 (p...e)，自然流露的 (s...s)

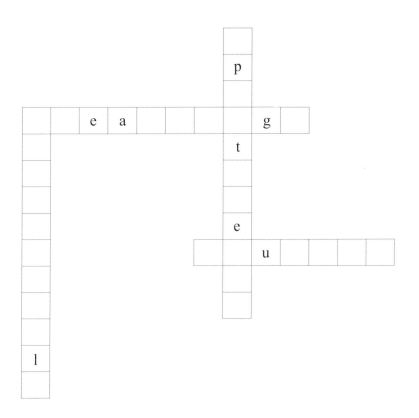

2. 必要的 (m...y)，壓力 (s...s)，貧困的 (n...y)，正面之事 *n.* (p...y)，促使 (e...e)

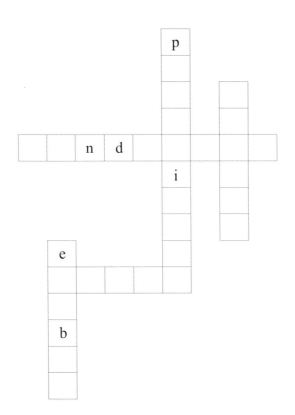

答案

一、填充

1. hone, specialty

2. accumulating, experiences

3. interpersonal relationships

4. Family, main focus

5. child's, carefree

二、Crossword Puzzles

1. `Across` prearrange, journey

   `Down` predictable, spontaneous

2. `Across` mandatory, needy

   `Down` enable, positivity, stress

珍惜苦難

最純淨的金子是用最猛烈的火提煉而來。

每一個人的生命就像夾了雜質的礦石,都要提煉,才會精良。

所以,**如果我們曾經身世坎坷,可以此為傲、昂首闊步,善用這份非凡的資財!**

如果我們現在的命運正處坎坷之際,沉住氣,並從容突破困境,想想最精良的金子從何而來吧!

Words of Wisdom

Adversity leads to prosperity.
　　逆境　　　　　　　興旺

Cherish Hard Times

- -

The finest gold can only be refined[1] with the hottest fires. Life is like a piece of rough ore[2] that needs to be refined.

Everyone goes through hard times. What sets people apart is how they react. Think about where fine gold comes from. If you fight and thrive[3] through tough[4] times, you can always walk with your head held high.

重要字彙

① refine [rɪˋfaɪn] (v.) 提煉
② ore [or] (n.) 礦
③ thrive [θraɪv] (v.) 興旺
④ tough [tʌf] (adj.) 堅毅的

逆境使我們更好

　　被揹上山的人，在自己走下山時，覺得辛苦不堪。但是辛苦走上山的人，卻可享受下山之時的輕鬆愉快。

　　最美的山景、最新鮮的空氣、最炫爛的彩虹，以及最皎潔的月光，都出現在大雨之後。

　　被豢養的動物放回森林時，生存堪慮；而從小在森林與苦難中長大的動物，則早已練就一身的本領，可以自行生存。

　　苦難造英雄，逆境是化了妝的祝福，不要妄自菲薄。

Words of Wisdom

Adversity and loss make a man wise.

Adversity Leads to Prosperity

Those who are carried to the top of a mountain are weak and unprepared[1] when it's time to hike[2] down on their own two feet. Those who walked up a mountain on their own build their muscles and train their bodies so that they can come back down quickly and easily.

Some of the most beautiful vistas,[3] freshest air, most dazzling[4] rainbows, and cleanest moonlights only come after torrential rains.[5]

Home-raised animals are scared and their safety is at stake when they are put back to the wild. By comparison, those who grew up in the wild are experienced and tough.

Adversity[6] builds character. Get through a tough situation, and you will come out stronger. Adversity is often a blessing in disguise.[7]

重要字彙

① unprepared [ˌʌnprɪˋpɛrd] (adj.) 沒準備好
② hike [haɪk] (v.) 登山
③ vista [ˋvɪstə] (n.) 景色
④ dazzling [ˋdæzlɪŋ] (adj.) 耀眼的
⑤ torrential rain [tɔˋrənʃəl ren] 豪雨
⑥ adversity [ədˋvɝsətɪ] (n.) 逆境
⑦ disguise [dɪsˋgaɪz] (n.) 偽裝

笑看人生起伏

不會有無盡的苦難，也沒有永遠的得意，因為不管是哪一種上坡，都有下坡；哪一種下坡，都將觸及平地。

不管如何陰雨綿綿，都會天晴。

不管掌聲如何雷動，都會歇止。

好友可能成為仇人，仇人也可能成為好友。

人生如跑馬燈，好壞日子輪著轉。

生命中，除了真理，沒什麼是不變的。

帶著微笑，面對順境與逆境。微笑至終的人，才是生命的真正贏家。

Words of Wisdom

While you're enjoying prosperity, be wary of adversity.

留意

Smile Through the Ups and Downs of Life

Good times don't last forever and neither do bad times. For every uphill there's a downhill, and every slope always leads to flat ground.

No matter how long it rains, the sky will eventually clear.

No matter how loud the applause[1] is, it will eventually stop.

Good friends may become enemies and vice-versa.

Except for the truth, nothing is persistent[2] in life.

Life is what you make of it. Make the best of things and smile through both the good and bad times.

重要字彙

① applause [ə`plɔz] (*n.*) 鼓掌
② persistent [pə`sistənt] (*adj.*) 持久的、有毅力的
persistence [pə`sistəns] (*n.*) 毅力、耐久

善用成功也善用失敗

如果你終於成功了，恭喜你，因為並不是每個聰明努力的人都能成功，所以請感恩！然後請你去幫助人。什麼都愈用愈少，只有愛才會愈用愈多！

如果你遭受挫敗，也不須懷憂喪志，因為失敗本來就是生命的一部份，它使我們看到自己的弱點和缺失，愈來愈有智慧！

如果再三失敗，我們也試著微笑以對——努力的本身，就已值得尊敬。何況，**人生何處不留遺憾**？

Words of Wisdom

The two hardest things in life to handle are success and failure.

Enjoy Success and Learn from Failure

If you find success, congratulations! You are blessed. Be grateful. Because life is unpredictable[1] and often unfair, not everyone who is smart or works hard will succeed.

Share your success with the needy. The only thing that increases the more you give it away is love.

If you encounter[2] a setback,[3] don't be frustrated. Setbacks will come and go. Most of the time they reveal shortcomings and mistakes, but sometimes they're completely out of your control. No matter what, setbacks will make you wiser.

Even if you fail repeatedly,[4] don't lose hope and don't stop smiling. No one and nothing in the world is impeccable.[5] Hard work is respectable in itself.

重要字彙

① unpredictable [ˌʌnprɪˋdɪktəbl̩] (adj.) 不可預料
② encounter [ɪnˋkaʊntə] (v.)(n.) 遭逢、邂逅
③ setback [ˋsɛtˌbæk] (n.) 挫敗
④ repeatedly [rɪˋpitɪdlɪ] (adv.) 重複地
⑤ impeccable [ɪmˋpɛkəbl̩] (adj.) 無瑕的

一、填充

1. 準備走下山了嗎？

   Ready to _____ _____?

2. 這道彩虹好炫爛喔！

   This _____ is _____!

3. 氣象局說，今天會有豪大雨！

   The Weather Bureau _____ says that we'll have

   _____ _____ today.

4. 患難造英雄。

   _____ builds _____.

5. 逆境是化了妝的祝福。

   _____ is a _____ in _____.

6. 生命難以預料，而且經常不公平。

   Life is _____ and often _____.

7. 不是每一個聰明人都會成功。

   Not _____ who is smart _____ succeed.

8. 和有需要的人分享。

   Share with _____ _____.

9. 他正遭逢一個挫敗。

   He is _____ a _____.

10. 挫敗多半顯出了我們的短處和錯失。

Most _____ _____ our _____ and

_____ .

二、crossword puzzle

請將以下所提示的英文單字填入字謎：提煉 (r...e)，礦 (o...e)，繁盛 (t...e)，堅毅 (t...h)，有益的 (a...s)，毅力 (p...e)

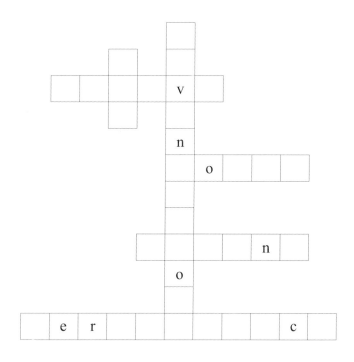

答案

一、填充

1. hike down

2. rainbow, dazzling

3. forecast, torrential rains

4. Adversity, character

5. Adversity, blessing, disguise

6. unpredictable, unfair

7. everyone, will

8. the needy

9. encountering, setback

10. setbacks, reveal, shortcomings, mistakes

二、Crossword Puzzle

1. **Across** thrive, tough, refine, persistence

   Down ore, advantageous

國家圖書館出版品預行編目資料

翻譯大師教你讀英文 / 郭岱宗作. -- 初版. -- 臺北市：
貝塔, 2011. 04
　　面：　公分

　ISBN: 978-957-729-831-7（平裝）

　1. 英語　2. 讀本

805.18　　　　　　　　　　　　　　100003234

翻譯大師教你讀英文

作　　　者／郭岱宗
插 畫 者／水腦
執行編輯／朱慧瑛

出　　　版／貝塔出版有限公司
地　　　址／台北市100館前路 12 號 11 樓
電　　　話／(02)2314-2525
傳　　　真／(02)2312-3535
郵　　　撥／19493777 貝塔出版有限公司
客服專線／(02)2314-3535
客服信箱／btservice@betamedia.com.tw

總 經 銷／時報文化出版企業股份有限公司
地　　　址／桃園縣龜山鄉萬壽路二段 351 號
電　　　話／(02) 2306-6842

發　　　行／智勝文化事業有限公司
地　　　址／台北市100中正區館前路 26 號 6 樓
電　　　話／(02)2388-6368
傳　　　真／(02)2388-0877

出版日期／2011 年 8 月初版三刷
定　　　價／280 元
I S B N／978-957-729-831-7

翻譯大師教你讀英文
Copyright 2011 by 郭岱宗
Published by Beta Multimedia Publishing

貝塔網址：www.betamedia.com.tw

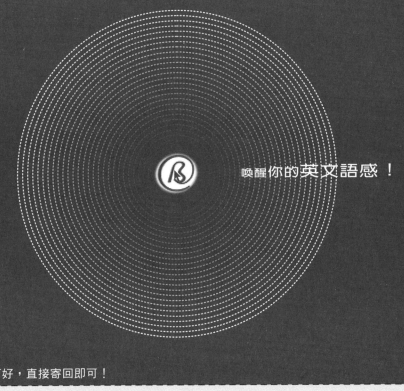

喚醒你的英文語感！

請對折後釘好，直接寄回即可！

100 台北市中正區館前路12號11樓

 貝塔語言出版 收
Beta Multimedia Publishing

 寄件者住址 ☐ ☐ ☐

貝塔語言出版
Beta Multimedia Publishing

讀者服務專線 (02) 2314-3535　讀者服務傳真 (02) 2312-3535
客戶服務信箱 btservice@betamedia.com.tw
www.betamedia.com.tw

謝謝您購買本書！！

貝塔語言擁有最優良之英文學習書籍，為提供您最佳的英語學習資訊，您填妥此表後寄回（免貼郵票），將可不定期免費收到本公司最新發行之書訊及活動訊息！

姓名：＿＿＿＿＿＿＿＿＿　性別：□男 □女　生日：＿＿年＿＿月＿＿日

電話：(公)＿＿＿＿＿＿＿＿(宅)＿＿＿＿＿＿＿＿(手機)＿＿＿＿＿＿＿＿

電子信箱：＿＿＿＿＿＿＿＿＿＿＿＿＿＿＿＿＿＿＿＿＿＿＿

學歷：□高中職含以下　□專科　□大學　□研究所含以上

職業：□金融　□服務　□傳播　□製造　□資訊　□軍公教　□出版
　　　□自由　□教育　□學生　□其他

職級：□企業負責人　□高階主管　□中階主管　□職員　□專業人士

1. 您購買的書籍是？＿＿＿＿＿＿＿＿＿＿＿＿＿＿＿＿＿＿＿

2. 您從何處得知本產品？（可複選）

　□書店 □網路 □書展 □校園活動 □廣告信函 □他人推薦 □新聞報導 □其他＿＿＿

3. 您覺得本產品價格：

　□偏高 □合理 □偏低

4. 請問目前您每週花了多少時間學英語？

　□不到十分鐘 □十分鐘以上，但不到半小時 □半小時以上，但不到一小時
　□一小時以上，但不到兩小時 □兩個小時以上 □不一定

5. 通常在選擇語言學習書時，哪些因素是您會考慮的？

　□封面 □內容、實用性 □品牌 □媒體、朋友推薦 □價格 □其他＿＿＿

6. 市面上您最需要的語言書種類為？

　□聽力 □閱讀 □文法 □口說 □寫作 □其他＿＿＿

7. 通常您會透過何種方式選購語言學習書籍？

　□書店門市 □網路書店 □郵購 □直接找出版社 □學校或公司團購 □其他＿＿＿

8. 給我們的建議：＿＿＿＿＿＿＿＿＿＿＿＿＿＿＿＿＿＿＿

＿＿＿＿＿＿＿＿＿＿＿＿＿＿＿＿＿＿＿＿＿＿＿＿＿＿＿

＿＿＿＿＿＿＿＿＿＿＿＿＿＿＿＿＿＿＿＿＿＿＿＿＿＿＿

喚醒你的英文語感！

Get a Feel for English !

喚醒你的英文語感！

Get a Feel for English !